PETTY, DEADLY, Gorgeous

Book Cover: Haelah Rice Designs

Formatting: Designs by Del

This is a dark romance that features the following: blood-play, breath control, torture, serial un-aliving, cannibalism, graphic descriptions of sex, violence and gore. In these pages you'll meet reincarnated people who live in a supernatural place and a demon who's an incubus.

IF ANY OF THIS OFFENDS OR DISTURBS YOU – please close the book and go about your day.

You've been warned.

Love,

Ivy

xo

Petty Deadly Gorgeous Playlist

Sweet Dreams
Marilyn Manson

Can't Find My Way Home
Blind Faith

I Put A Spell On You
Creedence Clearwater Revival

Darkside
Neoni

More Human Than Human
White Zombie

Sympathy For The Devil
Guns N Roses

Dance With the Devil
Breaking Benjamin

Blood
In This Moment

All The Beauty
Mortal Love

Omnis Mundi Creatura
Helium Vola

There Will Be Blood
Kim Petras

Blood
Dropkick Murpheys

Don't Fear the Reaper
Blue Oyester Cult

O'Death (Haunted Version)
Bobby Bass, Lauren Paley,
Colm McGuiness

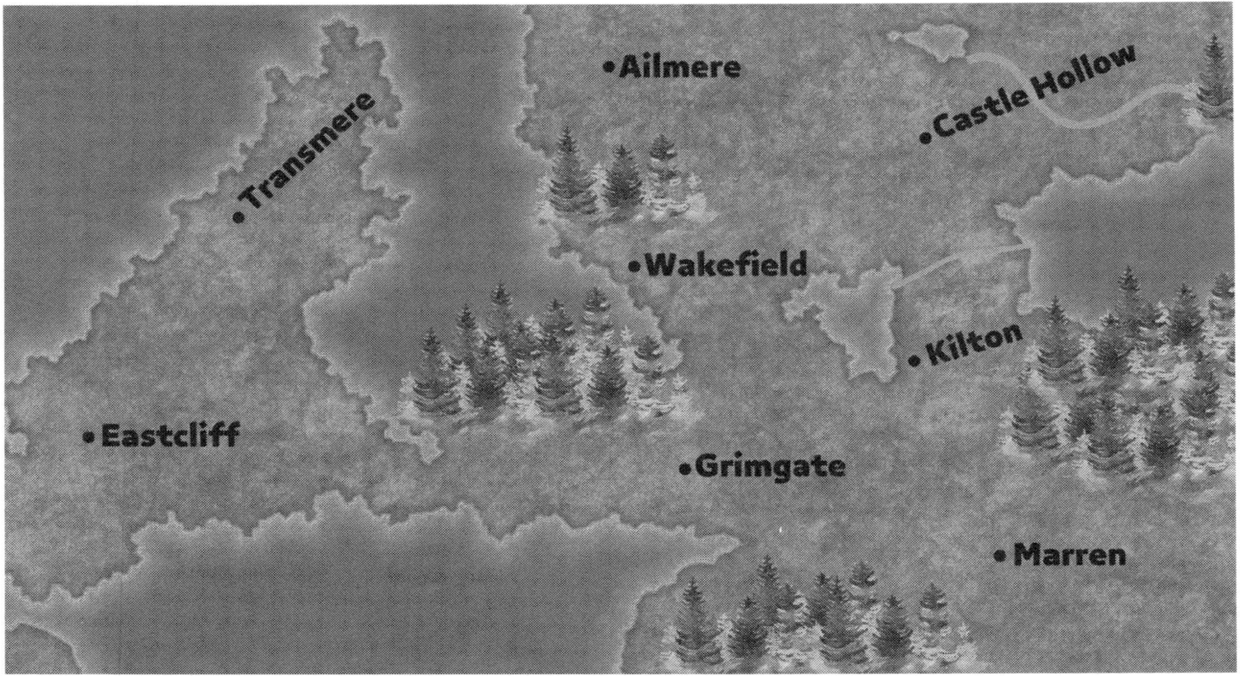

Ailmere
Castle Hollow
Transmere
Wakefield
Kilton
Eastcliff
Grimgate
Marren

CONTENTS

Prologue

Anna

I smiled at the young girl chained in my basement. Her tears flowed silently down her cheeks, and I couldn't resist cupping the soft skin of her face and using my thumb to feel the wetness.

"We all have a purpose in life." I crooned to her. "Yours is at hand."

"Puh... puh... please." Her bottom lip trembled. "Please let me go."

"I promise, I will release you soon." I leaned in and licked the other side of her wet face. "Now be a dear and let me work in peace today."

The ball gag I used to keep her silenced previously sat on the small table to my left. I removed it to feed her breakfast, and now it was time to put it back in place. Her head jounced, rattling her chains as I tried to insert it. She kept her lips pressed together tightly, leaving me no choice but to cause her pain.

Not that I minded causing any of my special girls pain, I loved hearing their screams and seeing them beg and cry fueled my lust.

Here in the basement my leggings and tee shirt worked well enough to keep part of me warm. My blond hair was swept up into a messy bun on top of my head, I smiled at the girl as my icy fingers flicked her nipple before pinching it in a hard twist. Her mouth fell open as she moaned in pain, and I crammed the gag in place to mute her. She could scream tonight before the ritual while we play with her.

"If you would've been good, I wouldn't have had to hurt you." I tapped the side of her face growing harder with each pat. Her body shook with tremors as I secured the gag in place. Drool seeped around the ball and seeing her lovely body this way gave me a rush of lust.

"Soon, my dear. Soon" I nodded and left the basement, switching off the light leaving her in darkness.

I had potions to mix, hex bags to make, and tarot readings to do. I didn't need any distractions today.

Anna

13 years old

Tonight for my birthday my mom and grandma are taking me to a special class with them. It's a reincarnation hypnosis class and I can't wait to see what other lives I've lived!

My family wasn't like other families. We didn't go to church; we didn't worship a single deity; we didn't even do the silly holidays others did. Some of the kids at school didn't understand, but others did because their families celebrated what they called Pagan holidays.

I liked the Pagan holidays, dancing around a maypole, trading Yule gifts, leaving out gifts for the Lord and Lady. It made me feel special, like we were part of something bigger.

I sat quietly at my dressing table and finished styling my long blond hair, taking care to set the curling iron back on the special mat to protect the antique wood. My mom loved antiques, and she made it a point to furnish our house like it was the turn of the century. She always reminded me that things weren't made like they used to be and we should take care of what we have.

Looking into the mirror in front of me, I stared at my reflection. My dark eyes never needed much to make them stand out. I still took my time doing my make-up. All day I felt like something magical would happen, so tonight I wanted to look perfect when I stepped into the class.

I wanted people to see me as an adult, not some silly child.

My reflection in the mirror had me looking behind me at my bed. Mom told me it was a bed fit for a queen, and when I inspected the intricate headboard and posts, I finally understood why. Whoever crafted this bed did it by hand. They carved it special for someone. Perhaps they were royalty. Whoever had it before me took care of it, and now I had to do my part.

Chores sucked, but I took my time dusting and cleaning my furniture, pretending to be a servant to a queen, and I needed to be sure she approved of my skills.

My eyes slid to my reflection again, taking in the deep red velvet bodice, embroidered with gold stars and symbols. It hugged my newly formed curves and made my small breasts stand up high.

Instead of the servant, I pretended to be a queen. I blinked my eyes and touched up my mascara, lifting my head high. Mom and dad thought my new gown from Gran looked too grown up for me.

Pffi. Peasants.

My eyes rolled back in my head, hearing them fighting downstairs with Gran about it while I finished getting ready.

"This fighting is silly, Jamie, and beneath you." Gran snapped.

"You need to step out of this and let me and Vivien work things out, Ramona." I heard something slam. "Now."

The silence that followed carried an eerie edge with it, and I heard footsteps on the stairs.

"I'm done with this bullshit magic thing you do, Viv." Glass broke and his voice raised. "I'm the god-damn head of this house."

The sound of skin slapping skin resonated before I heard my mom fight back. "Now? Jamison? Now you decide to assert yourself? You knew who I was when you fucking married me!"

Suddenly, my bedroom door opened, and Gran slipped in, holding an odd book to her chest. She closed the door and let out a sigh. "Silly fight, really."

"They always fight about this." I frowned and turned in my vanity chair. "Dad thinks mom practices witchcraft."

Gran walked over and sat on my bed and blew out another hard breath. "Magic gets such a bad rap." Her old hand patted the seat beside her. "Come see what I've brought you."

The air crackled and felt thicker as I moved to sit beside her. She placed the heavy book in my lap and my fingers lightly traced the bumps and lines on the cover. It immediately drew my eyes to it, admiring the soft fleshy color. “What is it?”

She stroked her hand down the back of my head. “Ah, my precious, this book has been a treasured heirloom handed down since the fifteen hundreds.”

Awe filled me as my fingertips flattened and my entire hand caressed the cover. “Is this real leather?” The book felt lighter the longer it sat in my lap and reminded me of a vintage scrapbook. The pages all seemed to be different sizes, making the book bulky.

“Of a sort.” She tilted her head and smiled at me. “Go on, open it up.”

Excitement filled me as I cracked open the cover. The same spark I felt earlier sizzled in the air and crazy as this sounds the book called to me. My eyes scanned the first page, and the writing felt familiar. In my soul I knew I’d seen this before.

The parchment paper inside should’ve looked old, but it didn’t and the writing on the page shifted and moved. I didn’t know what language they had written in it, but now the words were as recognizable as any book I’ve ever read.

Ink stood out deeper in places. Each page had a title, recipe list and instructions, only these were nothing like the recipes I’d seen before. Whatever this would make wasn’t something you’d serve for dinner.

It wasn’t until the third page I realized this wasn’t a cookbook. This book contained spells handed down from generations. Notes were scribbled in the margins, clearly done by different people. And in between some pages, they had tucked extra spells in.

There were drawings and samples of herbs and flowers for reference. Love. Money. Revenge. Each page held secrets on how to craft the perfect spell.

"Has mom seen this?" I whispered softly as I continued reading over each page.

"Of course. It's a family heirloom." Gran stood from the bed. "She chose your father over old family traditions."

"Gee. That worked out great." I huffed, hearing my dad's booming voice echoing through the house.

"Put it someplace safe." She gave me a wink. "Away from prying eyes."

I closed the book and smiled. "Thank you, Gran. I love it."

My mother rejected this gift, but I couldn't wait to read more and learn what my ancestors knew.

"I knew you would, Anna."

Downstairs, more glass hit the wall and shattered, followed by my mom screaming. "FUCK YOU, JAMISON BISHOP!"

With a shake of her head, gran slipped from my room, and I followed. Her voice spoke in a dangerous, calm tone. "That's more than enough. Today is Anna's day, and here the two of you stand fighting like school children. You should be ashamed."

"Ramona, I told you. This is between me and Vivien." Dad growled back.

Gran's fists balled up, and she stomped her foot. "Bljai laidogoro oarliz ourro!" The lights flicked, and I heard my mom scream.

My eyes grew wide and awe filled me. "What was that?"

"Mother! You cannot just do that to him!" Mom spun and stomped her foot in anger at Gran.

"I can. And I did." Gran turned to me. "*That* was magic."

"Anna, spellcasting isn't not to be toyed with." Mom's voice trembled as she spoke and her eyes glanced sideways at my dad. "Mom, please?"

Gran let out a sigh as she turned back to my mom. "Vivien, gather your things. We have a class to attend with Anna. This is her celebration. Your piece of shit husband is just paused. He'll be fine while we're gone, then you can continue this silly fight and Anna will spend the night with me." She shook her arms down and turned to me. "Ready to go, darling?"

I watched mom walk out of the room, and I walked over to my dad. My hand twitched as I touched his cheek. When he didn't move, I waved my hand in front of my father's face. He didn't blink. The awe I felt grew as my dad stood still, not breathing or moving. I looked over at Gran. "Can I learn to do this?"

Her laugh filled the room. "My dear, you will learn that and so much more."

I always felt like a misfit, but now? Now I think I knew where I belonged. *Tonight should be epic!*

“I’m ready.” Mom came back into the room, putting her jacket on. “I’m sorry, Anna, Gran is right. This is your night and we shouldn’t have been fighting.”

I shrugged, slipping into my jacket. “No offense, mom, I’m kinda used to it.”

“Hmph.” Gran snatched up her jacket and walked out the door, letting it slam behind her.

“We should go.” I sighed and went out after her getting into the car. Mom joined us a few minutes later, her eyes swollen from crying. She started the car and pulled out of the driveway, heading for the community center.

We could cut the tension in the car with a knife. This wasn’t how I wanted my birthday to go. I thought as a family we’d all do something fun.

“Mom?” I sat forward between the seats to be closer to them. “Why does dad hate witchcraft so much?”

“Anna, witchcraft is nothing to play with. People can get hurt. There’s always a price for magic.”

Gran chuffed. “That didn’t stop you your freshman year when you cast the spell for Henry to ask you to prom.”

“Mother.”

Laughter bubbled up from me. “Mom, you really cast a spell?”

“Oh, not just one. Back before your father, she was quite the caster.”

Mom’s shoulders relaxed, and a small smile graced her face. “Jamie doesn’t understand, and sometimes people are afraid of what they don’t understand.” She pulled into the parking lot. “He said he needed to know that he loved me without interference and, for that to happen, I *chose* to put magic aside."

Gran's eyebrow raised. "*Your* father never worried about that."

As mom pulled into a parking spot and shut the car off, she tilted her head and gave gran a glare. With a shake of her head, Gran raised her arms in defeat and together we all got out of the car and went inside the community center.

We walked into the main room, finding all the people attending in small groups chatting away. I took time to look around at everything. Someone stacked all the tables to one side of the room and there were soft mismatched couches placed around. Against the back wall, you could find drinks and snacks and a large sign pointing the way to the restrooms.

I knew almost everyone here. They were from all walks of life, and we were all here for one reason. We all wanted to know what lives we lived before. There were no other children here, only me. That made me puff my chest out with pride.

As I strolled through the room, I said hi and thanked people for the birthday wishes and compliments. I loved living in Castle Hollow and the people here. Diversity made our town special and the acceptance of that made it better than any other place I've visited.

I rubbed my toe at a stain on the carpet, wondering what could've caused such a spot. Mister Graves lifted his water glass at me as I looked up and I smiled at him. His restaurant had the best barbeque in town.

Gran and mom were deep into a whispered conversation. I'd never seen them at odds like this before. As I walked closer to them, brief phrases caught my ears like *he is forbidding Anna to learn* and *he's still pissed that you taught her how to read tarot* and *tend a witch's garden*.

Anger welled inside my chest.

What right does he have to be angry at Gran? Even if I don't learn now, I'll just learn it later.

A vision of the magic book Gran gave me flashed in my head.

YES! I'll find something in there when I get home to change his mind.

A loud, deep, strangely familiar voice filled the room, and I looked over to see the most handsome man I'd ever seen in my thirteen years. "Let's take a seat and get ready to travel!"

Hoops and hollers followed as everyone found their places. I locked my eyes onto his built body. Jeans clung to his hips and legs, outlining his package, which made my eyes widen. Boys at school never looked like that. His tee shirt hugged his torso, showing off a defined six-pack, and his nipple poked up. His lips were full with a perfect cupid's bow, the kind all girls dream of having and their color reminded me of fresh meat. A perfect reddish-pink.

Green eyes accentuated with dark lashes sparkled with his own excitement, and I felt a pit in my stomach. Mom told me all about stranger danger, but I *wanted* to be dangerous. I wanted to sit in his lap and see how he compared to the magazine my friend Julie snagged from her mom's room with all the naked men in it.

My ears strained to hear every word. Not that he wasn't talking loud enough. I wanted to hear the little breaths between each word of his low, purring voice.

"Welcome to our past life regression class. I'm Jon and my assistants have some pillows and blankets to hand out and they are yours to take home." His eyes locked onto mine as he continued. "Tonight it's my hope that you find peace and comfort as you travel back into locked memories to find who you were."

"Excuse me, Jon?" Gran interrupted. "How many past lives can we hope to discover?"

He winked at her, and jealousy filled me. "Well, some have one and some have many, but the most important and relevant one will come to you first. You can choose to explore that first one in depth or hop around."

A hand flew up on the other side of the room. Miss Martha bounced in her seat. "Do we need to share with the class afterward?"

Jon gave a snigger, and his chest bounced. "Of course not, Miss Martha. This is all for you to learn about you."

"Anyone else?" His eyes met mine, and he winked. My stomach tightened, and I felt my vagina quiver like when I watch porn without my parents noticing.

The assistant handed me a soft pink pillow and a matching blanket as my hand flew up in the air.

"Yes, Anna?"

He knows my name!

"What if nothing happens?" My voice trembled in anticipation.

He gave a soft laugh, not the nasty one he gave Martha, and the sound made my stomach clench tighter. "Don't worry, I'm sure you'll all have an experience you'll never forget." He kept his eyes on mine but asked the room again. "Any other questions?"

When no one said anything more, he snapped his fingers and pointed at the light switches. "Let's dim the lights. Please get comfortable either sitting up or laying down and once I see that everyone is comfortable we'll begin."

I tried sitting up, then laying back, but neither position worked. "Can I move to a different place?" I whispered to Gran.

"Of course, Anna." She smiled and made herself comfortable.

My eyes scanned the room, looking for a place where I could be alone. I noticed a couple of gray bean bag chairs tossed in a corner that looked like the perfect place for me. With my new pink pillow and blanket in hand, I made my way over to them and dropped to the floor. I adjusted the chairs so I could prop my legs up on one and used the other for some privacy before tucking the pillow under my head.

All the sounds in the room slowly died down, except for Jon's footsteps as he walked around the room.

"This room is our safe place. I want you all to focus on your breathing. Deep breath in and slowly release it. Let go of your doubts." His deep voice softened, sounding like a soothing whisper in my ear. "Let go of any anger. It's just you. Me. And darkness of the room."

A smile stretched across my face, thinking about it being only me and him. I spread the blanket out over my body and rubbed the soft material between my fingers.

"In and out. Just breathe. There's nothing else here. Leave your earthly body where you are and let your spirit float. Let it glide along current memories and then let it go to find the answers you seek. Set it free with your breath in and on your breath out. Look at the you from long ago."

Just like he told me, I filled my lungs and let my lips part slightly to let the breath out. The more I focused on my breathing, the lighter I felt. Almost like the game light as a feather that we tried at my friend's slumber party. Each deep breath made me feel like I could float.

His voice held the same tone and cadence as he spoke. I swore it felt like his lips were against the shell of my ear. A tender reminder to relax and let go. I trusted him and, deep in my soul, knew he would never do something to hurt me.

Another breath in and I felt a breeze over my skin. My breath out, I let go of the fight from earlier. Deep breath in and the air tasted different. I released the breath and saw myself laying there. As I turned, I saw a mirror in front of me at the end of a long hall.

Darkness flooded my field of vision, and I could see only the mirror. I walked toward it, breathing in and out, feeling my chest tighten. My eyes looked down, noticing instead of jeans, there was a skirt. I couldn't feel my blanket or the rough carpeted floor.

My hands shook as I reached down, smoothing down the fabric. Wetness met my fingers, and I continued my scan up over my hips to the ornately corseted bodice. They embroidered gold threads to accent the darker fabric. My breasts were full pushing up out of the top and my cleavage was deep. The dress fabric reminded me of a couch in a museum. And as I lifted my head, my eyes peered back at me. Instead of seeing a young child, I saw a beautiful woman.

Dark eyes blinked and looked up at the hat on my head. My hair was tucked up under it, and my lips looked painted red. My eyes stared back at me, but my nose looked sharper, my cheekbones were more defined and my face shape felt different.

Who am I?

I looked back at my hands, taking a deep breath in, and a strange yet familiar metallic scent filled my nostrils.

Two young women walked towards me. They both bowed and kept their eyes averted.

I'm royalty! I must be a princess!

"Countess, your offering is ready." One spoke quietly, still not looking at me.

I tilted my head and looked at her dowdy servant's dress and as she glanced up to see what I was doing; I knew her name in an instant. "Ilona."

"Yes, ma'am."

I motioned with my hand. "Lead the way."

She's my servant, but where are we going?

She and the other woman took a few steps from me and my eyes adjusted to the light in the room. The dimly lit room showed a fancy bed and dressers, a couch, and some chairs. And they made the walls of bricks.

I took my first steps after them and saw more of the cold, dark bricks as I left my bedroom. Tapestries lined the walls and torches were interspersed, lighting the way.

I'm in a castle. And I'm the Countess.

My head lifted higher, expanding my chest against the confines of the bodice, and a smile grew on my face. The sound of my heeled shoes clicked on the floor, sounding powerful. I slowed my steps to look at each of the tapestries and the scene unfolding before me. They intermixed pastoral scenes designed to bring relaxation, with ones showing victories of war.

We made our way down the hall to a set of stairs. I stood there for a brief moment, marveling at the torches on the walls, lighting the way down and the shadows they cast on the wall. My hands clutched my skirts, holding them up so I wouldn't trip on them, and my belly filled with butterflies of excitement as I descended upon them. I didn't know where we were going, but I had a feeling it would be extraordinary.

At the bottom of the stairs, the servants were running around. None of them made eye contact with me. They bustled around, appearing busy as we made our way through an incredibly large room. An enormous table sat in the middle, two fireplaces flanked it and a fresh scent joined the metallic one.

Maybe fresh wasn't the right word. It reminded me of the woods after it rained. Wet, moldy and mostly unpleasant. Some people were sitting there eating, having quiet conversations, and merely dipped a nod in my direction.

They led me through the room, through the kitchen, where wonderful smells assaulted my senses and cooks scurried about. From there, we entered the servants' wing and traveled that hallway to a heavy door. Upon opening it, I saw more stairs that spiraled to the lower parts of the castle. We continued down these stairs and the closer we got to the bottom, the stronger the metallic scent.

I lifted my head as I took the last step and saw a young girl chained in the middle of the room. Her thin body stretched, pulling her to her tiptoes. Naked. I unapologetically pushed my way between the servants and walked to her. Tears streamed down her dirty face, and she shook harder the closer I came to her.

They placed mirrors around the room. As I glanced in one, I could see everything. They were there so I could watch every movement. My hand reached for her cheek, cupping it, letting my thumb stroke the softness. From there, my hands moved to her throat and clutched around it, watching her gasp for air. I felt that fluttery feeling in my belly again. This time, my pussy spasmed with it.

A moan slipped from my lips. “Yes, you’ll do nicely.” I smiled and released her throat, taking a few steps back.

Ilona and Dorotya, I remember the other one’s name, stepped over and unchained her, letting her fall to the floor. They left her there and went to light more torches on the wall, illuminating the area completely. Dorortya came back to the young girl with a tool in her hand and I heard a loud cracking sound before the young girl cried out in pain.

“Again.” I commanded.

Dorotya nodded at me and I watched this time as she broke another of the girl’s fingers with a tool in her hand.

“Faster. And her toes too.” I bit my lip in excitement.

They did exactly as I bid and I felt fingers working on unbinding my corset. Breath against my neck raised goosebumps and his voice was in my ear.

“I see you found yourself again, my queen.” A tongue licked my ear. “You have been so missed.”

My voice came out breathy. “Jon?”

“That’s one of my many names.” He nipped my ear and pushed my corset off. His hands ripped the rest of the gown from my body, leaving me naked and chilly. “I can smell your excitement.”

“I ache.” He pinched my nipples as I leaned back against him.

“What shall we do with her?” He crooned against my ear.

An evil laugh rose from my chest. “Stand her up.” Together, we walked closer to her as the girls lifted her to her feet. I licked my lips and leaned forward, taking her nipple into my mouth, sucking hard before biting down on it to taste blood. I pulled my mouth off with a pop.

"Is it bath time, Countess Elizabeth?" Ilona smiled softly at me.

My eyes grew wide, and I walked out of Jon's embrace to pick up my dagger from the small table off to the left. This room had a special purpose. Torture, sex and bloodbaths.

"I never want to be an old crone." I licked the blade, tasting the old blood on it, then walked closer to tonight's offering.

The young offering shook her head violently. "No. No. No. No. No. No."

"Oh sweet girl, yes."

Her eyes were wide in horror. "Countess Bathory, please."

"Please?" My voice mocked hers. "Now you wish to be polite?"

"I... I'll do anything."

My head fell back as I laughed. "Darling, you already are."

I placed the blade at her neck and watched as Jon went around behind her. His hands groped her breasts, and he ground his hips at her back. He wet his finger in her blood and traced it down to her pussy, shoving his finger in.

Her pretty little mouth fell open in a moan, and she barely struggled against my servants' hands, panting with each pump of his hand.

"Look who's a little slut?" I popped the t on the last word and traced the blade of the dagger along my body, delighting in the slight pain I caused myself. "Is her heart pumping hard?" I licked my lips.

He winked at me. "She's ready."

I stepped closer, feeling her flesh against mine. I gave a nod, and he yanked her head back hard, allowing me to slice through her neck swiftly. "At daluku nue, usthai enca ciili hisii!"

Her blood pumped out between us. Together Dorotya, Ilona and Jon lifted her, allowing me to bathe in her warm, sticky life force. My dagger clattered to the ground as I rubbed it in, over my breasts, between my legs, and over my face.

The metallic scent made sense now, and my mouth watered, craving more. They watched as I enjoyed this sweet gift, even as I masturbated, spreading her blood on my vagina. My spell to stay youthful worked all over my body and when no blood ran from her; the girls carried her to a cell in the back and Jon stepped closer to me.

"Here you're an adult. Back there, you are a child."

"And?" I reached out, grabbing his cock in my bloody hands. It throbbed between my palms and I stroked it, delighting in the pleasure he received from it.

A loud clapping snapped me back to my body, and I felt wet. My hands moved to my face and came away covered in sweat. Not blood.

Holy shit! I was... no. I AM *Elizabeth Bathory.*

Anna

My heart pounded in my chest, and my head spun. I wanted to be horrified by what I saw, but my body hummed in excitement.

All around me were murmurs of joy and people sharing their experiences. Gran and mom looked at me, and for a moment I couldn't breathe.

What do I tell them?

I scanned the room to find Jon. He motioned to the hallway beside him and then disappeared down it. My hands were clutching my chest, holding my beating heart, willing it to slow down.

I glanced back over to mom and Gran and they were both smiling and holding hands, talking. I motioned to the hall where the bathrooms were and they both gave me an understanding nod. My legs felt like rubber as I stood up and rushed over to the hall.

My steps slowed when I didn't see him anywhere, and I turned my back to the janitor's door. "Jon?"

The door whooshed open, and arms pulled me inside before closing the door for privacy. "My beautiful Countess."

My mouth opened slightly, and I gasped. "It was real."

His large hands cupped my face tenderly. "Absolutely."

"We know each other?" I nodded as a warmth traveled through my body. The urge to go to him and wrap my arms around him grew stronger by the second. "You don't feel like a stranger to me."

"I'm not." He dropped to his knees. "I've been your humble servant for centuries."

I stared at him on the floor, and my hands trembled as I cupped his face and lifted it for examination. His skin had no blemishes, no flaws I could find, and felt like satin beneath my fingertips. His green eyes were unusually green, like peridot gems that had just been polished but had veins of gold in them.

A small button nose sat above those perfect cupid's bow lips and I leaned in to kiss them. My first kiss! I sighed as I pulled back and felt my head spin.

My eyes scanned the small room filled with overflowing metal shelves of towels, trash bags, mop heads, gloves and chemicals. I took a couple of steps back and took a deep breath, tasting the cleaning supplies in the air. Underneath, I could smell a sweet mint. It's a scent I knew well as I could smell it in my bedroom late at night and anytime I felt overwhelmed or afraid.

"The mint..." I leaned against the shelf beside me, causing the products to rattle. "That's you."

God, I want to hug him.

"Yes." He nodded and sat back on his heels.

My head tilted down and took in the man on his knees before me. "*What* are you?"

I don't care what he is. I feel safer than I ever have in my life!

He lifted his head and a sly smile crossed his face. His eyes went black. "A demon called to this world by you."

"I?" My throat felt tight as I swallowed. "Me? I called you into being?"

"You." A seductive tone tainted his voice. "Late one stormy night, your husband was off doing whatever it was he did and you wanted to get laid. You cast the circle and called an incubus into being to be your slave. Your lover."

Sex? With him? My pussy needs to stop twitching.

I blinked and pushed back against the shelf. "An incubus?" I felt the tremble in my body from my toes to my hair as he opened his arms to me.

"My sweet, please, I know this is overwhelming. You're usually much older when you learn who you are and who I am."

Tears made their way down my cheeks. "I thought incubus only slept with sleeping women? That's what I read when we studied mythology."

Has he done that? Has he taken me in my sleep?

"Usually yes. But..." He casually lifted a shoulder in a half shrug. "Once a demon comes into being, we can do other things as well."

"I'm so confused!" I wrapped my arms around myself. "I shouldn't have enjoyed killing that woman! I shouldn't have wanted more! And I shouldn't want to be close to you! I don't even know you!"

Yes, you do, dummy.

He motioned with his hands for me to come into his waiting arms, and I couldn't fight the feeling of going to him anymore. As soon as he could reach me, he pulled me close and held me as sobs shook my body. I let myself nestle into the safety of his arms. And the tears kept coming. He rocked us, murmuring softly in my ear. "There, there, my love. Let it out."

I don't know how long we were there, hiding from the outside world. His powerful arms protected me from everything. And then I heard my mom's voice.

"Have you seen Anna?"

"She's in the bathroom." Agnes responded in her usual monotone. "Let's go back to the room."

"Thank you, Aggie. She probably needs a moment."

Once the hall became quiet, I looked up at the man holding me. "Jon?" I shuddered, drawing in a breath. "Thank you."

"Always." He pressed a kiss to the top of my head, then leaned me back and reached up to dry my tears. "You should sneak into the bathroom and fix your makeup before rejoining the class."

I couldn't help whispering. "Will I see you later?"

"Call me, and I will be there." He brushed the hair from my face and kissed my forehead tenderly.

"Are you my first?"

"First for what?" He smiled.

"Sex."

"No." His rich laugh filled the room. "You've never given me that honor."

"Hm." I smiled. "Maybe it's time for things to change?"

"Temptress." His low voice caused my skin to prickle up in excitement. "Not now. You are far too young."

My eyes rolled back in my head as I stood up from his lap and shivered at his missing warmth. "Pfft."

I left him sitting on the floor as I cracked the door open and peeked outside to make sure I could sneak out and over to the bathrooms. Without looking back, I entered the empty hall and jogged to the bathroom. Once inside, I leaned against the door and took three deep breaths.

Questions filled my head, and I couldn't wait until later to ask him. I also couldn't wait to look at my new spell book again. I went to the sink and splashed cold water on my face, then cleaned up the smudged mascara before joining everyone in the common room again.

Jon stood with a group chatting as I slowly passed by on my way to Gran and mom. My mom opened her arms and drew me close, hugging me tight. "Well? What did you learn?"

"I was royalty."

Mom squealed and gave me a tighter squeeze. "That's wonderful, darling!" And I heard her whisper. "See, Mom, no magic."

Gran rolled her eyes and then smiled at me. "Fancy gowns, servants, big castle?"

"Yes. It was overwhelming." I sighed. "Can we go home?"

"Don't you want to share your experience with others?" Mom pulled back and looked down at me.

"I thought you were worried about Dad?" I looked up as innocently as I could.

Mom's eyes closed, and I felt her stiffen beside me. "Dammit."

Gran laughed. "Already forgot about him?"

"Mother." She growled at Gran.

"Fine. Let's go. Anna can get her things and come back to my place tonight as planned."

We gathered our things and slipped from the building out to the car. The ride home felt intensely quiet. No one spoke. We all sat in silent contemplation.

I couldn't stop thinking about the feel of the warm blood coating my skin, and the way the peasant seemed to enjoy being touched by the demon. Even the servants had smiles on their faces, delighting in each moment.

Another memory slid into my vision. I saw a man leaving. He lined the servants up to send him off and he pecked my lips. The kiss left a pit in my stomach. I couldn't wait for his cold, scratchy lips to move.

"I promise to be back within a fortnight." He cupped my face, but the touch didn't feel soft.

"Of course, darling." The words came from my mouth, but not my young one. I could hear the change in my voice and language and knew I stood there as the Countess.

We watched him climb into the carriage as the driver commanded the horses to move. Once they cleared the gate, I turned to Ilona. *"I feel like playing a game tonight."*

She bowed, and with a wave of my hand, I dismissed them all.

"Anna?" My mom's voice broke through the memory. "Are you coming inside?"

I shook off the vision and smiled. "Of course!"

After getting out of the car, I walked in to see Gran, waving her hand, saying one word. "Iroeshru."

"You need to stay out of it." Dad spoke as though no time had elapsed. He glared at mom. "I guess go to your hypno-whatever class and we'll finish this later."

Giggles bubbled out of me. "Daddy, we're back."

His face went pale, and he turned to Gran. "What. Did. You. Do." He enunciated each word with more anger and hate than I'd ever heard from him before.

"You're fine." She shrugged and looked back at me. "Anna, go get your things."

"Oh, no!" He roared. "My daughter is NOT going with you."

"Daddy?" I felt my face scrunch up. "It's my birthday. I want to spend it with Gran."

"No." He looked me dead in the face. "You are not leaving this house with her."

"Jamie, let's talk about this." Mom stepped up and he slapped her.

I stepped forward but Gran held me away with her hand as we watched mom clutch her cheek in astonishment. Mom snapped her head back and glared at him.

"Anna Elizabeth, go get your things." Her eyes remained on his face, and I knew she was sending me out of the room.

"Mom..."

"Anna Elizabeth. Now."

I blew out a frustrated breath and ran up the stairs to my room. Hot tears streamed down my cheeks as I grabbed my backpack and filled it with pajamas, my overnight kit, and a change of clothes. Anger roared in my ears and I tuned out the fighting downstairs.

How dare he hit her! No man should ever hit a woman. Not like that. Not in anger! What is his deal?

The book Gran gave me whispered my name. I felt it call to me and I dropped to my knees and pulled it from between my mattress and box spring. It felt warm to the touch, and I clutched it to my chest.

This wasn't any spell book. I made it centuries ago with that young girls' skin for a cover.

"Holy shit!" I dropped the book and scuttled back. My eyes blinked rapidly. "It's not leather."

Anna.

My hand shook as I reached for the book.

Yesssss. Anna.

I lifted the book and brought it back to my chest, cradling it. The book wanted to be near me, and I wanted to be near it. I tucked it into my backpack and raced back down the stairs. Gran stormed through the back door and my parents stood there looking at each other.

Worry filled me. "Where's Gran going?"

"To her car to wait for you." Mom muttered.

"We're letting you go tonight, Anna, but tomorrow before you come home, you need to tell her goodbye." Dad looked at me with a slight smile on his face.

My eyes narrowed. "What do you mean I need to tell her goodbye?" I turned to my mother. "Mom? What is he talking about?"

"Anna, your father and I decided that it was best if you don't see Gran for a while."

"No." He pursed his lips. "We decided it was best to not see her again."

I stood there, slaw-jawed, shaking my head in denial.

"When she's eighteen, she's going to do what she wants, Jamie."

"Not under my roof."

"Hold on." I held up a hand at each parent. "Better for who?"

"All of us." Dad smiled. "This is what we need to do to protect our family from her and that bullshit witchcraft."

I felt bile pushing its way up my throat. "Mom?"

"Anna, someday you'll be marr..."

"NO." I stomped my foot. "How could you turn your back on your mother?"

A single tear dripped from her eyes. "I have to do what's best for my family."

"She *is* your family."

"Anna, we call the shots. Not you." Dad went to the fridge and pulled out a can of beer. "You'll go tonight, say goodbye tomorrow and that will be the end of it."

"The hell it will!" I snapped.

Mom's hand popped out and across my face so fast I couldn't breathe, causing me to drop my backpack to the floor. "You will not talk to your father that way."

My teeth bit into my skin inside my mouth until I tasted blood. My nostrils flared, and I pursed my lips. "I'm going to Gran's."

"Have a good time. We'll see you tomorrow."

Oh, you'll see me tomorrow, all right. For the last time.

I picked up my bag and stomped to the door, and let the door slam behind me. There wasn't anything left to say to them. As I opened the car door, I slid into my seat and saw Gran wipe the tears from her face.

"I'm sorry, Gran." I reached for her hand and held it in mine while we drove in silence across town to her bed-and-breakfast inn. She didn't have any guests, so our time tonight would be for us.

It broke my heart that she couldn't speak. My parents were being unfair to her and me, and they didn't give two shits. We drove past the community center and saw there were still some people milling about.

"I..." Gran sniffled. "I hope the class was good for you."

"Oh Gran. I'm so thankful I went to that class tonight." I gave her hand a small squeeze.

Now that I know who I am, I know what I needed to do to stop my parents from being assholes.

Gran squeezed my hand back and gave me a wane smile. She made the last turn and drove up the road to the Serene Raven Inn. The inn had been in our family for decades and gained attention from all over. Some said ghosts haunted it. Some said magic lived there.

Our family had a small gift shop inside it where you could find potions, hex bags and Gran did tarot readings. Sometimes she even let me do readings. I liked the money I made from it and a child who could divine their future fascinated people.

She pulled up the long drive and parked in the carriage house. Her expression as she faced me fueled the anger inside me.

"Let's go in." I smiled.

She nodded, and we got out of the car and went inside, entering through the backdoor that led to the kitchen. I watched as she put the kettle on to make some tea. Sadness warred inside me with anger. Being here in Gran's house, this is what home should feel like. And if my parents weren't in the way, this would be my home. A soft sigh left my lips as I took the back stairs to put my bag up to my room.

The old stairs creaked when you stepped on them just right, but after all the years I've spent here, I knew where to step to avoid that. The front staircase was my favorite. It had solid wood banners, wide steps, and they were carpeted.

The ones from the kitchen were so the workers could deliver room service to the clients. And for the family to use as we needed to let the clients staying enjoy their stay without us interfering. At least that's what I've always been told.

My foot hit the top landing with a stomp, and I ran the short distance down the hall, ignoring the paintings and tables to my room. Anger bubbled up in my chest, as I dropped my bag and grabbed my pillow, screaming into its soft muffling safety.

I could kill them for wanting to take me from Gran.

My fingers continued to clutch the pillow, and I ripped it in half as a plan formed in my head. I wanted to live here, with Gran. To learn and grow with her. Mom and dad fought all the time and I couldn't take it anymore. I wanted peace.

Anna.

The soft voice floated to my ears, and my knees dropped to the hardwood floor as I pulled the book from my bag. My fingers tingled, feeling it in my hands, and I flipped through the pages, scanning for the right spell.

Love, no. Money, no. Beauty, no. Erase memories, no.

I looked up and scanned the room; I loved my antique metal bed, and the way the mattress cradled my body. All the furniture in this room I handpicked. The veneer covered wardrobe, long dresser and the set of bedside tables where I set my books that I read in bed.

"There has to be something to help me in here." I growled and a tiny slip of parchment drifted out to the floor. I shifted the book in my hands and looked down to see what fell out. A devious smile passed over my face as I read the title of the spell.

Freeze and see, yes!

I sat back and picked it up to read what the spell did and squealed as I read: *paralyze your intended so they can see what you are doing. They won't be able to move or speak.*

Perfect.

Once Gran falls asleep for the night, I can sneak out and go home to work my magic and show my parents the pain they've caused. It should be easy enough to be back before anyone knows what I've done.

Gran's old orange tabby strolled into the room and rubbed his head on me. I bit my lip, gave Cosmo a scratch on his chin, and spoke in a hushed whisper. "Uoqka pol pairo."

My hand trembled as I touched his side and gasped when he didn't move. His amber eyes blinked, and I looked back at the paper for the command to undo the spell.

"Iroeshru."

Cosmo shook his head and smacked me with his paw before turning and flicking his tail in irritation at me.

"I'm sorry, Cos, I needed to try it out."

"Mew." He left the room, and I smiled bigger.

I successfully cast my first spell.

I tucked the parchment back inside the book and set it aside so I could pull out my pajamas and shower before having a cup of tea before bed. Thoughts swarmed in my head. The sense of power I felt, the slick, warm blood. And the urge to touch myself after seeing her naked, feeling her nipple in my mouth!

Stumbling to the bathroom, I set my water and stepped inside. Once the shower curtain closed, I let the water wash away the anger and disgust I felt with my parents. *How dare they ruin my birthday!* My head was back, letting the water penetrate through my thick hair, and I rotated my head around in a circle.

My PE teacher, Aggie, taught us this move to relieve stress in your neck and shoulders. I scrubbed my body from head to toe and then got out, wrapping a towel around me.

After drying my air with my small towel, I combed it out and split it down the middle so I could braid both sides. I rubbed my sweet rose scented lotion all over my body before slipping into my jammies and then went downstairs to the kitchen.

Gran sat at the table, talking with Jon. "There you are, darling." She motioned me over. "Mister Dixon came to see how you enjoyed the class."

My head tilted, and I felt my nipples tighten.

He came to see me!

I walked over and made myself a cup of tea and then sat beside Gran. "Hi, Mister Dixon."

"Ladies, please, call me Jon."

"Jon." I giggled.

His cheeks turned red, and he looked down at his cup of tea. "As your Gran said..." He glanced up at me, his green eyes sparkling. "I wanted to see how you enjoyed the class and if I could answer any questions."

"Because I was once someone. Does that still make me them?"

He tilted his head. "Give me an example?"

"Let's say you were King Tut in a past life. Are you still King Tut, just in another body? Or are you Jon Dixon, who once lived as King Tut?"

"Gotcha." He winked at me. "If that were my life, I would in fact be King Tut in this new body of Jon Dixon."

"So I'm a Countess in a child's body?"

Gran laughed. "Exactly."

I let out a soft sigh and sipped my tea before a yawn took over.

"It seems my sweet Anna is happy with her past life." Gran got up and tossed her tea bags away and rinsed her cup. "You'll need to excuse us, Jon. It's been a long, excitement filled night."

"Of course, ladies." He nodded and did the same with his cup. "Don't hesitate to call me if you have questions or need anything."

Gran patted his shoulder and almost pushed him out the door. "Let's get ready for bed. I'm beat. We can get up early and have some fun."

I had my plans for tonight already. I just needed a quick nap to allow everyone to fall asleep. We climbed the stairs and Gran tucked me into my cozy bed. As she bent to kiss my forehead, I not only saw but felt the deep pain she tucked away.

Don't worry, Gran. No one will separate us.

Anna

Sleep came easily after the events of the night, and I woke up before my alarm went off.

I slipped from my bed and put my jeans and hoodie on before creeping down the hall to the main stairs. These stairs didn't creak, making my escape easier. I focused hard on my footfalls; I needed to move slow but swift. There was no need to call attention to myself.

I knew where every piece of furniture sat, which made sneaking around them in the moonlight a piece of cake. I clung to the shadows. Around the settee, between the buffet and the back of a rocker, and then a left to make my way into the kitchen.

The table sat slightly off to the right, and I reached my hands out to feel the backs of the chairs and then slipped between the backside of the table and the counter. Five steps to the door and I turned the handle slowly, pulling the door open in itty bitty motions to avoid it squeaking.

I blew out a hard breath and opened the screen door, pulling the heavy wood door closed behind me. The sweet scent of mint floated to me and I paused.

"And where do you think you're going?" Jon's voice came from the darkness.

"I need to take a walk." I looked around me. "Where are you?"

The air shimmered, and he stood to my right. "I'm here."

I huffed a frustrated breath and walked away from him.

"Where are we going?" He jogged and caught up with me.

I shook my head and made my way to the back of the estate. To be successful, I couldn't be seen. And I didn't need some adult tagging along.

His firm hand wrapped around my wrist. "Anna. Where are you going?"

"Jon, I need to take care of something. And I need to do this alone." I rolled my eyes at him. "Let me go."

"You know who you are to me. Let me help."

"No." I gave my arm a yank, to no avail. "This is a me thing."

"Countess." His voice dropped an octave.

"If you are who you say you are, give me this." I huffed. "Show me I can trust you."

We stood there in the darkness staring each other down and finally he relented, letting my hand go. I left him standing there as I slipped around a sign and disappeared from sight. Twigs snapped, leaves shuffled and my breath came out in puffs.

The inn wasn't far from my home. I only had to make it five blocks over and into the house. This isn't the first time I snuck back home. I had to do this a few times last school year because I forgot my schoolwork. And if dad would've known, he would've said no more sleepovers on school nights.

Stray cats darted here and there between houses and garbage cans joined by the occasional armadillo and opossum. As long as I ignored them, they ignored me and before I knew it, my house came into view.

No lights on. Perfect.

Experience taught me that after a fight like tonight, my parents wouldn't be sleeping in the same room. I dodge the line of sight for the motion-activated light and slipped into the house undetected.

Soft laughter hit my ears, and I tiptoed towards the sound. Around the island in the kitchen, and spreading my legs wide to step on the far edges of the stairs, I made my way up to the second floor.

"Jamie!" Mom laughed and moaned.

What are they doing?

I took a deep breath and slowed my steps down the hall, past my room, to the room at the end of the hall. They didn't close the door and soft light illuminated the room. Light I never would've seen from outside.

When I got to the doorway, I saw them wrapped up together, naked, trading kisses.

How could she kiss that man after he hit her?

"Mom?" The disgust and shock I felt tainted my voice.

"Oh, my god! Anna!" She sat up and tried to cover her breasts. "What are you doing home?"

"I hate you!" My voice filled the room as I screamed and then threw my hand towards them. "Uoqka pol pairo."

Both of them blinked, but neither moved.

"I came to talk sense into you, *Mother*." I sneered. "You think I don't know what sex is? I know. And I know that having it with a man who hit you and barred you from seeing your own mother isn't right!"

The look in her eyes changed from shock to horror, and I smiled.

Good, she should be afraid of me.

Mint wafted in the air, and I heard a voice in my ear. "Would you like her to speak?"

I nodded my head and waited. She blinked tears aways and her voice was hoarse.

"Anna, I need you to understand. Magic is dangerous."

"You can't be serious. Dad was fine when he was unfrozen from time."

"There are other spells that will cost more, possibly even your soul." She swallowed. "I'm begging you, Anna, please do as we ask."

"If I stay away from magic, can I see Gran?"

"No."

Turning on my heel, I left the room and ran to my bedroom. There in a box under my bed, I had my special dagger. Gran called it an athame. The blade glimmered in the moonlight, and in my hand I knew what its purpose was.

The room felt like a carousel ride as it spun around me, making me dizzy. My body trembled, and I closed my eyes to calm the swaying. Memories flooded back, ways to hurt, torture, and have fun with people. All the options that flashed in my mind in rapid succession were different, and time felt frozen. I don't know how long it lasted, but when it was over I opened my eyes, stood and went back to my parents.

"Father? Can you speak?"

He swallowed as mother had before we could hear his hoarse voice. "Precious, I just want what's best for you."

"No. You want what's best for you."

"Anna, I don't want to see you burn in hell." His eyes hardened. "And that's what is going to happen if you pursue this path."

I barked out a laugh. "No father. I won't burn in hell." With slow steps, I walked towards the bed, then climbed up to kneel before my parents. My head tilted to the side, and I reached for my father's mouth. "Your mean words hurt, Daddy." I pouted.

"I... I'm sorry, baby."

Holding my athame up in the room's moonlight, I smiled. "Not yet, you're not. But you will be." My tongue stuck out, and I licked the clean blade. "Stick out your tongue."

"Anna, stop being ridiculous." His voice shook even though he gave it a firm edge.

I poked the blade into his shoulder, watching in delight as it pierced his skin and blood oozed down around my blade. "Stick. Out. Your. Tongue."

"Young lady." He growled. "Knock this shit off right now."

More laughter bubbled up out of me as I pulled the blade out. “Hm, not cooperative?” In a swift, smooth motion, I twisted my body and stabbed it into my mother’s leg.

“Anna!” she screamed and gritted her teeth, panting in pain.

“Anna Elizabeth.” My father spoke low.

“You want her pain to stop? Stick out your tongue.” I batted my eyes innocently.

I watched in anticipation as his eyes flitted between me and the knife in his wife’s leg. Since he was taking his time doing what I wanted, I twisted the blade, making her cry out again and slowly he stuck his tongue out.

“That’s a good boy.” I patted his cheek with my free hand. “Keep it out.”

On a sob, I heard my mother ask. “Who are you?”

Ignoring her, I reached for his tongue, cringing when I felt its slimy texture making me growl as it slid through my fingers.

Hm, this won’t work.

I looked at the bedsheet and pulled it up, wrapping it around part of his tongue so I could pull it out further. Once I had it out as far as it would come, I pulled the athame from her thigh and brought it to his soft muscle that was wiggling in my fingers.

“You’ll never tell me what to do again.” My knife sliced through and blood pooled in his mouth and dribbled down his chest. “You’ll never speak a mean word to anyone again!”

"Help! OH MY GOD! Help!" My mother's voice grated my ears and my hand flew back, slapping her hard with dad's tongue still clutched in my hand.

"Shut. Up. Mother." I let go of dad's tongue and grabbed more of the bedsheet, shoving my fingers into her mouth. "Give me yours or I'll stab you in the heart and make dad watch as I draw in your skin."

I could feel her jaw trembling and she stopped fighting me, allowing me to pull her tongue out and slice it off the same way.

"You know?" Jon's breath warmed my ear. "Mister Graves would love those tongues."

"Really?" I felt my eyes widen. "Why?"

"He loves all parts of these ridiculous creatures." His finger softly traced down my arm.

"Maybe I'll wrap them as a gift."

Tears streamed down both of my parents' faces and I smiled proudly at my work. With a tilt of my head, I looked back at my dad.

"You know what, Daddy?"

His eyes blinked as more tears flowed. Now, instead of a stern father, he could play the part of a frozen mute until I finished what I started.

"I hated the way you talked to me." My hand plunged the knife into his thigh. "I hated the way you spoke to mom." I pulled it out and plunged it into his side. "And I really hated how you treated Gran."

My head turned to see my mother. "And you?" I pulled the knife from him and plunged it into her upper arm. "Allowing him to shove you, and hit you, and then you give him your cunt!" I pulled the knife out and thrust it into the bed between us. "Yes, mother, I know that word and many others. How could you turn your back on your mother?"

Her lips trembled, and blood poured from them.

"You both forgot I had feelings, too. Feelings that you both stomped all over with every fight you had! Feelings that were crushed with each new rule. But now? Now, I'll be with Gran. I'll learn everything she has to teach me."

My father groaned, and it really pissed me off. I pulled the dagger from the bed and stabbed it into his throat. "Just. Die." I twisted the blade and watched as life drained from his face.

"Tsk-tsk." I giggled and removed the blade. "Guess it's your turn, mommy." My laughter grew. "And with your blood running all over my body, I start my process of living forever and staying young and beautiful"

My bloody hand cupped her face. "You are giving me life. Isn't that wonderful?"

I plunged the blade into her neck, pulling it out and slicing across her throat like I did in my regression, and felt her warm blood wash over my hand. Leaning in, I hugged her to me so I could feel the rest drain. "Thank you, Mommy."

"My sweet Countess, you will need to clean up and have a change of clothing."

I lifted my head and I looked around. The bed contained most of the blood and there were no footprints.

"Jon? How do I not get caught?"

"Allow me." He gave me a gentlemanly bow. "Stay right there until I come back."

Doing as he said, I watched him leave the room, and felt myself growing cold as the blood cooled. I waited for the guilt of what I'd done to hit me, but it never came. I felt liberated! Intoxicated!

I wonder if this is what being drunk feels like?

Jon stepped back into the room. "Are you going to release them?"

"Oh, yeah!" I laughed. "Iroeshru."

Both of their bodies slumped down, and I groaned as I gave Mother a hard shove back. Jon disappeared from sight and a moment later, I felt a sheet wrap around me as he lifted me up in his powerful arms.

He carried me from the room, down the stairs and out of the house. My athame lay across my belly, safely poking away from him, and he followed the path into the woods. He shimmered into my vision and I leaned my head on his chest, inhaling the sweet mix of blood and mint. I felt my emotions rise peculiarly. Turning my head, I nuzzled his chest and pressed a soft kiss to his covered chest, and heard a soft growl.

His footfalls were gentle as he trudged through the floor of the woods, but he startled a deer that was nibbling ahead of us. She stood still and then dashed which made me smile and a soft sigh escaped my lips.

My voice sounded muffled against his chest. "I don't feel guilty."

"Why should you?"

"I just killed my parents."

"Ah, but did they deserve it?" He winked at me.

"I think so. Yes."

"Never feel guilty for doing what you feel is right."

The air changed from chilly to a warm moistness. The river should be near us, which seemed like the perfect place to get cleaned up. I thought he would put me down until I heard his feet splash into the water.

"Aren't you going to put me down?"

"Of course." He nodded and lowered me so I could stand.

Usually, the water wasn't that cold and tonight it felt just right. Stabbing the soft ground with my dagger, I let the sheet drop from around me and I looked over my shoulder at him.

"Don't get any ideas." He shook his head at me. "You have my whole heart and my devotion. That should suffice for now."

"Why?" I stomped my foot in the water.

"If anyone got wind of the fact that I touched you intimately, they would lock me up." His eyes hardened.

Damn him. He was right.

I felt the pout on my face and I blew out a hard breath. "Then you better turn around."

Groaning inwardly, I stripped down until I was completely naked under the moon. My feet carried me further into the water and I dove underneath. The water felt so good against my skin and I rubbed my body lightly. When I broke the surface, Jon cut a sharp whistle and tossed a bar of soap at me.

"Where did you get this?" I missed catching it and had to fish around for it.

"You had a bag packed already with it inside."

That made sense. I'd packed a bag to go to Gran's for last weekend, but dad found an excuse not to let me go. After finding my soap, I moved towards shallow water to scrub myself clean. I didn't see Jon anywhere, but clean pajamas laid out on a large rock.

Taking my time, I used the moonlight to guide me and help wash away any trace of evidence of my game tonight. Once I felt clean, I stepped from the water and shook my body like a dog trying to remove the excess water before slipping into the clean clothes.

My backpack sat beside the rock and I pulled out my slippers before dropping the soap inside along with my athame. Then I picked up my bag and followed the path back to Gran's. I needed a nap, a proper shower and some good home cooking from her.

I snuck back into the house and up to my room without notice and the moment my head hit my pillow, happiness filled me.

I'm home for good.

Dominick

Present Day

My office chair molded to fit my ass. This was both comforting and disturbing. “Memory foam, you say?”

“Dom. Stop being a pussy. They got us good chairs to keep us at our peak.” My partner Sean threw a ball of paper at me. “I like it.”

“I know what you like, man. That’s what scares me.” I laughed and threw the ball in the trash.

Together we were the best cold case duo our jurisdiction had. This morning while I assembled my new chair, the higher ups brought down a case from Castle Hollow. A young girl lost both her parents the night of her thirteenth birthday. After thirty years and no leads, they dumped it on us.

I glanced at the folder with the cold case and then turned my attention to another set of files in front of me. In this stack were the current cases of missing girls who either went to visit Castle Hollow or were near the area.

“You ever been out to Castle Hollow?” Sean asked while flipping through the dossier.

I leaned back and decided the chair was definitely more comfortable than anything else I've ever sat in. "No, but I've heard the stories."

It was hard to live near a tourist trap of haunted woods, buildings, and not hear all the rumors about the surrounding areas. People were superstitious and always looked for a reason to explain what they didn't understand or want to accept.

"We could go talk to the girl." He shrugged. "See what she remembers?"

"How much do you remember from thirty years ago?" I sat up and crossed my hands on the desk.

Sean's face twisted up, and he laughed. "Shit. Not much, except I was a fucking idiot."

"She was thirteen. And she wasn't even home."

He drummed his thumbs on his desk. "What are your thoughts on the missing girls?"

"I think it's fucking weird that the only thing in common is the age range." I reached for my coffee and took a big swig of the now cold swill. "But. The owner of the Serene Raven Inn is the same girl who lost her parents."

"Well, that's two birds with one stone if I ever heard one." Sean leaned over and pulled a quarter from his pocket. "Call it." He balanced the coin on his thumb and then flipped it into the air, catching it on the back of his hand.

I watched it flip and called out my choice. "Tails."

He uncovered it and frowned. "Dammit. Guess I'll go dig through thirty-year-old evidence."

"That means I'll go to Castle Hollow and meet Anna Bishop." I stood up from the chair and grabbed my blazer from the back, and picked up my copy of the files. I preferred an old wood desk to this new one, but they were trying to pull the station into this century.

The small coffee station still had the old wood desk, and I wondered for a brief moment if anyone would notice if I swapped them out. Shaking my head, I threw my blazer over my arm and left our office.

For a small area, we had a busy office, and there were people rushing around and others on the phones, all with their own cases to handle. I waved at the other officers as I made my way out of the station and down to my car.

I took a deep breath of fresh air and enjoyed the stillness outside the station. My mind drifted to the case. According to the reports I read, there was no weapon found, but the couple's tongues had been cut out of their mouths.

"That's not a bad plan if you want to keep your victims silent." I opened my car door and slid into the driver's seat. "But how do you get them to comply when there's no signs of a struggle?"

Sticking the key into the ignition, my car fired up, and I continued to talk to myself while I drove down the highway that would take me from Grimgate to Castle Hollow.

"Why wasn't there a struggle, though?" I reached over and lowered the radio. "If someone is trying to kill you, you fight for your life. It's instinct."

This cold case baffled me. Usually, after looking over the old case notes, evidence notes, statements, something would jump at us. Something that told us this was the place to begin the search. This time, there was nothing.

"Bupkis!" I slammed my hands on the steering wheel. "That's what we got. Bupkis!"

Dammit! My twenty years as a cop should be a huge help right now.

With a shake of my head, I leaned forward and turned my radio back up. Maybe some music would help me get outside of my head and give me fresh eyes to see what we were overlooking in the cases.

I heard the crack of thunder and saw spikes of lightning touch down.

How appropriate. I'm heading into a rumored haunted town, and the weather plays along.

It felt like time slowed as I rolled past the welcome to Castle Hollow sign. Leaves blew in the wind, fat drops of rain splashed on my windshield. I could see each one individually, and it reminded me of what I thought crocodile tears were as a kid.

An ominous feeling started at the top of my head and casually strolled over my body, making me shake.

"What the hell?" I looked from side to side and then focused out the windshield and, with a blink of my eye, time moved as though it never slowed down.

As I drove closer to Caste Hollow, the signs on the side of the road noted the change from the highway to Main Street. The community center came into view, beside it the post office and then City Hall. On the other side of the street, I saw a barber, salon, grocery store and a restaurant.

Then a sign for the Serene Raven, which sat back in its grandeur, calling your attention. I veered around the water fountain in the middle of town and drove up the long drive to the Inn.

The building itself reminded me of something straight out of a Hitchcock film. Old. Gothic. Spooky. But inviting. My eyebrow quirked up as I felt the strange pull to the inn.

"Stop being a superstitious pansy, Dom." I huffed a frustrated breath at myself and pulled into the parking area. "I wonder if Vincent Price will greet me at the door?"

Laughing at my stupidity, I shut off the car, grabbed my blazer, and climbed out. The grounds were impressive. Perfectly manicured lawn, sculpted trees, flowers in bloom. If I had time to take a vacation, this would be ideal.

I followed the path up to the sidewalk and then up the stairs to the door. A welcome sign hung to the left of the main door and I entered slowly, my eyes scanning and taking in all the décor. Inside felt as though I stepped through a portal back in time. Antique furniture filled the sitting room. To my right stood a coat tree with an umbrella holder.

"Haven't seen one of those in years." I mused aloud.

"That was one of Mistress Ramona's favorite pieces." A deep male voice resonated through me. Lifting my head, I looked around and soon saw a young man walking my way. "Welcome to the Serene Raven."

"Thank you." I nodded and stared at his unnaturally bright green eyes. "I am looking for Miss Anna Bishop."

"Of course." He smiled. "May I tell her who's come calling?"

"Dominick Moody."

"Don't you mean officer?" He winked at me.

My head tilted as my eyes narrowed. "Detective."

"Apologies, Detective." He gave me a bow and turned on his heel.

Once he left my sight, I went back to surveying the room. It reminded me of my great-grandma's living room. No television. One large picture window and several small ones with heavy drapes, plants placed strategically to get the best light and seating for everyone to be included.

Behind me stood an old oak counter that served as the front desk with a fancy internal mailbox system on the wall organized with keys. I took a few steps over and strolled down the hallway to a small shop that reminded me of how hippies smell.

Shelves lined the walls, conveniently at eye level height, with small drawers beneath them. My shoes clicked on the old wood floors as I wandered over and opened a drawer up to find neatly organized soaps that matched the display.

"Are you needing something to moisturize your skin? Or something to draw a special someone closer?" A smokey woman's voice came from behind me.

"Actually, I was just sating my curiosity." I closed the drawer and turned to see who joined me. Years of being a cop helped me keep my face neutral as I took in the beauty standing there.

Thick blond hair piled high on her head in a messy bun, exposing a long, elegant neck. Shapely legs hugged by leggings that left nothing to the imagination and a cropped tee shirt sporting the inn's logo. As she shifted her weight from one leg to the other, the shirt moved, exposing the tiniest sliver of her pale skin.

"You know, curiosity killed the cat." She flashed me a bright white smile.

Smiling back at her, I gave her a cheeky wink. "Ah, but satisfaction brought him back."

Her head fell back in laughter and I stepped closer with my hand out. "I'm Detective Dominick Moody."

Her small hands met mine and instead of shaking, she turned my hand palm side up and her icy fingers traced the lines. "Hm, rebel at heart, good life line, rocky love life." She tipped her head and smiled at me again. "Pleasure to meet you, Detective Moody."

My blazer and shirt hid the goose bumps that rose on my skin. "I'm investigating the disappearance of some girls in this area and wondered if I could show you their pictures?"

"Of course. Could I get you a cup of coffee or tea?"

"Coffee sounds delicious." I nodded and waited for her to lead the way.

She turned on her toes like a ballerina and walked ahead of me. Her hips swayed seductively, keeping my eyes locked on the fullness of her plush ass.

What is wrong with you, Dom?

I wasn't a man who lusted after women. *Pffi, just ask my ex-wife.* She's more than happy to tell anyone who'll listen how unromantic and lack-luster of a lover I am.

She walked around a corner, and we entered the main kitchen. The young man who greeted me motioned to the table for us to sit and he placed a tray on the table, complete with a carafe of coffee, a teapot, a small creamer pitcher, and a sugar bowl.

"Would you care for some homemade maple donuts, Detective?" His soft voice caressed my skin, and I felt weird having my dick half hard between these two.

"Sure." I shrugged and took a seat, adjusting myself under the table.

Anna poured me a cup of coffee and the man brought me a small plate with a large donut. She turned her attention to making a cup of tea for herself and then looked up at him and gave him a wink as she dropped in a sugar cube.

She stirred her tea slowly, and I felt her eyes on me. "You said you had some photos?"

"Yes." I pulled them from the inside of my blazer and slid them across the table to her. "Are any of them familiar?" I took a bite of my donut and moaned at the taste. "This is *really* good."

A soft laugh left her lips. "Thank you. It was my gran's recipe." She spread the pictures out and looked at each one, shaking her head with a sigh. "No, I'm sorry."

After taking another bite, I took a drink of my coffee and then turned to the young man, doing dishes. "What about you, Jon?"

He dried his hands and came back to the table, looking over her shoulder. "I have to agree with Anna." He looked up at me, his face unreadable. "None of them look familiar."

I sat quietly, finishing my donut, then I took another drink and tapped the fingers of my free hand on the table. "Do you have any guests who have been here long enough that I might ask?"

"Sorry, no guests right now." She scrunched her nose up and took another look at the photos. "They're all so different, don't cases like this usually have an em oh?"

"CSI watcher?" I joked with her.

She laughed and took a sip of her tea. "Forensic Files."

The storm outside picked up, and the thunder rolled harder and louder. Rain beat against the windowpanes and as I glanced over, I noticed how the darkness had rolled in.

"Hm, I think you might need to hunker down here with us tonight." An apologetic smile passed across her face. "No charge."

"I'm not afraid of a little rain." I reached for my photos. "But I do need to talk to you about something else."

A siren went off, and Jon laughed. “Bet there’s a limb down. I’ll head out and see if I can help.” He leaned down and brushed a kiss across her lips.

“Be safe, darling.” She cupped his cheek and watched him leave through the back door. Once we heard the car leave, she turned her attention back to me. “Now we’re alone. What can I do for you?”

Anna

Holy hotness!

The man sitting in my kitchen is far from what I think of when I think of detectives. He's young, thick dark wavy hair, ocean blue eyes and his hands felt strong when I checked them out.

I bet those would feel amazing wrapped around my throat.

I watched as his eyes filled with skepticism and I knew my kiss with Jon confused him. "Jon and I are very open, Detective Moody." I refreshed his coffee. "Now what was it you needed to talk with me about other than the missing girls?"

His face relaxed, and he sat back in his chair. "When you were thirteen..."

"Ah. My parents' deaths." I nodded, schooling my features to show sadness. "It's been so long."

He studied me. I could feel his eyes searing into my soul, looking for any crumb he could find. His blue eyes were welcome to gaze upon me as long as he wanted.

From the moment we met, I felt his lust and taking him to bed would be a delight.

I swallowed hard, pulling energy to play my part. A small sigh left my parted lips, and I refilled my teacup. "Let's get comfortable for that talk." Picking up my cup and saucer, I motioned with my head as I stood for him to follow me.

His chair scraped the floor as he scooted back, and I heard his footfalls as he trailed behind me to the front parlor. I skirted around a recliner and set my saucer down on the coffee table before turning and holding my hand out for his blazer. "Allow me to hang that up for you. You'll be more comfortable."

"Do I need a coaster?" He nodded to the table.

"No. It's a piece of furniture to be used, not pampered."

After he set his cup down, he shrugged out of his jacket, showing off his shoulder harness and giving me more to look at before handing it to me. I could still feel his eyes watching me as I moved away from him to the coat tree and back. He waited for me to sit first and I smiled at him again. "So gentlemanly."

He chuffed and adjusted his tie. "I assure you, not everyone thinks so."

"Then they're wrong, Detective." I tucked my leg under my body as I sat down in the corner, cocked to face him. "What would you like to know about my tragic birthday?"

He sat back on the couch and crossed his left leg over the top of his right, with his ankle resting on his knee.

His pink tongue darted out and wet his lips as he looked over at me. "According to the report, you found your parents."

Crossing my arms, I rubbed my hands on the upper part and nodded. "Yes. I spent the night here with my Gran. In the morning, we had a massive breakfast of all my favorite foods and then I walked home. I remember the sun shining, the birds chirping and the strange smell when I entered my home."

"Strange how?"

My lips twisted as I thought for a moment. "Metallic." I scrunched my nose up. "Raw sewer or rotting vegetables?" I nodded. "Yeah, that was mostly what I smelled. It was bracing and unforgettable."

"I'm sorry you had to experience that at such a young age."

I reached up and wiped a tear from my eye. "Thank you."

Silence hung between us. He sat forward to get his coffee, cleared his throat, and took a drink before asking his next question. "Did you touch anything in the house?"

"No. I dropped my bag on the kitchen floor and ran through the house, looking for them. When I reached the end of the hall and saw them there, naked, bloody, on the bed, I screamed." I fanned my face to keep the tears from falling. "I remember the neighbors' arms around me, pulling me from the house and then police and medics."

"I'm sorry. Do you need a minute?" His eyes looked genuinely worried for me.

"It's just such a traumatic event." I sniffled and got up to get some tissues from the small table next to the recliner. "And even now, no one knows *who* would even want to hurt my parents that way!"

I dropped into the chair and held my head with my hands and let the tears flow. Dominick sat forward on the couch with his elbows on his knees, letting go of a sigh. "We haven't given up, Anna. We're still working on the case."

"Tell me, Detective Moody, do these cases get solved after almost thirty years?" I sat up to meet his gaze and blew my nose. More tears fell like the rain down my cheeks.

"Sometimes we get a break and yeah, we solve them."

A loud clap of thunder rumbled through the house, showing all the storm's fury as the wind howled and shoved the trees around outside.

I wrapped my arms around my body and nodded to the window. "This storm is getting worse. You may want to call your wife, and let her know you're staying here."

A small smile cracked his stoney demeanor. "There's no wife to call."

"Boyfriend?" I raised an eyebrow, teasing him.

"Not the team I bat for."

I knew how to play up a man, and I knew what it would take to get him to fall under my spell. Closing my eyes, I opened them coyly and smiled at him. "Never?"

"Not even once." He sat back, his smile growing cocky. "Men just don't..."

Standing up, I walked over and sat beside him, my hand on his thigh. "Funny, I thought your pants looked fuller when you were talking with Jon."

He cleared his throat and scooted into the couch further. "Is there anything else you can tell me about your parents' murder?"

Laughter howled inside me, while my face showed nothing of my joy.

"Sorry to disappoint you, Detective Moody." I moved my hand up an inch. "But no. Nothing else stands out."

The cocky smile waned and his features returned to what I perceived to be their standard place, and he gave me a nod. "I'm going to call my partner and since I have time on my hands..." He stood up and straightened his tie. "I think a nap would suit me well."

My tongue poked from my lips, wetting them before I stood up and brushed against him before walking to the check-in desk. "I think you'll find room thirteen to your satisfaction." I slid the key from the mailbox to him, daring him to touch me to get it.

Like a moth to a flame, his hand covered mine after taking the bait.

"Up the stairs to the second floor, turn left and it'll be on your right." My voice deepened, infusing a honeyed smokiness. "Call if you need... anything." I tilted my head and smiled. "I serve dinner around sex." My mouth dropped open at my Freudian slip. "Oops." I snorted with laughter. "I mean six."

As he walked away, I leaned on the counter and watched. His slacks tightened with each step on the stairs, which highlighted a very firm, biteable ass. They did nothing to hide his cock when he fought against the lust Jon created by being in the room.

My shoulders rolled my shoulders as I let the lust wash over me. My sweet incubus brings that out in everyone. And I would bet that under the right circumstance, Moody would bust a nut for Jon.

"Hm." Deliciously devious ideas crept through my mind. All of them revolved around Dominick and his ass. Penetrating it, stretching it and watching Jon make him cry out when he lets go of his inhibitions. Feeling them both fuck me. And the best part? My intuition told me there was something dark inside of our fine detective. It just needed to be cultivated.

I let the images play in my head as I strolled to my pantry. This wasn't one's typical pantry. You wouldn't find dry beans, cans of fruit or jars of sauces for noodles. In this magical pantry, you would find everything one needs to mix up potions, tinctures, and hex bags.

My fingers tingled as I lifted the pestle from my mortar and sat down on my rolling stool. "Just a pinch of this." I sang and rolled myself to the other end. "And a dab of that. Let's not forget we want him to remember the night." Rolling back to the mortar, I dropped the herbs in and ground them. "Goddess, watch over me as I create this tasty boost for the dear detective. Guide me by your hand to show him the darkness he fears."

"Ah yes!" I set the pestle down. "We need a little something for relaxation." I got up and danced my way to the other end of the pantry until I found the jar of belladonna. "Not too much. Just a pinch."

I knew the moment Jon returned from helping. There wasn't a need to see him; I felt him. My heart ramped up and lust danced on my skin. A vision of me on my back, my legs wrapped around his handsome face, while I writhed on the kitchen table flashed in my head. I could feel the weeping of my pussy as my leggings caught the wetness.

Strolling back to the mortar, I dropped in the few crystals and left the pantry to meet Jon in the kitchen. He stood naked in the room, his hair wet from the rain, and for me, his tail twitched and pointed to the table.

"Mm, my lover." I purred and hurried to the table.

"Open wide." His low voice made my body tingle as I hopped up and opened my legs.

His long claws pranced along my seam, first gently, then I felt the sharp points tear at the cloth. Deep buzzing sounds filled the kitchen as he dropped to his knees, putting his face at eye level with my pussy.

One swipe of his forked tongue teased both lips and hugged my clit, giving it a tug. There's no containing the moans when he works me over in this manner. His claws dug into my skin, giving me a bit of pain I craved, and his tail plunged into my core, filling me fully.

Jon nips and licks at my cunt, teasing me. "He's handsome, yes?"

"Yeeeeesssss." I hiss and grind my hips towards his face.

"Dark in the core." His tongue swats against my clit, treating it like a boxing bag.

My hips lift off the table and pump against the movements of his tail. "Eat. Me." I pant. "Talk. Later."

Laughter takes the place of Jon's buzzing. I loved the feeling he added to the air and then the buzz came back with a force. Some incubus thump, some hum and some buzz like a bee. That strange buzz affected each person differently, but in the end, it filled them with pure lust.

I pushed my shirt up and grabbed at my nipples, twisting and pulling them. Jon's tongue hugs my clit and suckles it. Inside my pussy, I feel his tail move in and out and it bounces inside me.

His tongue tickles my clit as he speaks. "Yoh aah-hoe ip beppin por appenpen."

"Finger. Fuck. It." I growled and let go of my nipples long enough to grab his head and cram it as far inside me as I could. "But keep eating." My back arched up. "My pussy."

His finger wasted no time pushing into my tight ass, making swirls and moving deeper. His tongue held still inside me until his finger was all the way in and then he moved them like a teeter-totter in and out, sending my emotions up and down.

"Jon." I groaned and felt sweat covering my body. "I'm so close." I laid back on the table and he slowed his motions down. "What are you doing?" I yelled through gritted teeth.

He gave my clit a bite and pulled back. "You come when I say you do."

I feel my eyebrow raise at him. "Is that a fact?"

His head nodded slowly, and I felt another finger entering my ass. "Not a moment before."

"Jon," I pouted. "Please? That damn detective got me all hot and horny."

His fingers continued their assault on my ass, while his tail moved against them again. He stood and leaned over me. "I would love to see him tie you up." He wagged his eyebrows and sucked in a nipple.

A moan slipped out as I gasped. "You wouldn't."

"Restrained and face-fucked." He bit my nipple and licked at the tiny amount of blood that rose to the top. "Holding your head tight. Slamming his cock down your throat until you make him come."

My chest rose and fell in hard breaths. "Gonna make me swallow it all?"

"Every. Last. Drop." He leaned to the other side and bit the swell of my breast, making me bleed so he could lick it up once more. "And then you'll thank him for the honor." Jon bit his way down my body and licked my clit teasingly. "Now tell me what you want to see."

"I want to see him bend you over, hold you by your tail and fuck your ass until your nuts are bouncing together."

Jon's eyes sparkled, and his tongue went back to work on my clit.

"I want to watch you both jack off and squirt all over me and then I want to be in the middle while you both fuck me." I moaned and gripped the table, panting. "I want to ride him on the couch and feel those hands gripping my hair."

He squeezed my clit hard, and I cried out in orgasm, locking my thighs around his head. I cried out. "I'd let him top!"

My body trembled on the table, shaking it, and Jon's claws dug into my hips, holding me still as my body released all over his face. He let go of my clit, pulled his tail out and lapped at my juice, tickling me as I came down from an amazing high.

Dominick

Listening to Sean drone on as he caught me up on what he found in evidence had me kicking back on the bed and loosening my tie. I wasn't shocked to hear he didn't see anything new. I blew out a hard breath and filled him in on Anna. By the end of the call, we agreed something seemed very off in this case.

The storm raged harder as we spoke, and after disconnecting the call, I tossed my phone on the bed and leaned my head against the headboard. I closed my eyes and replayed the conversation with Anna back in my head. Her sultry voice, combined with her aggressive advance, intrigued me.

Most women steered clear of me. I knew why, but they didn't. It always got chalked up to having the male equivalent of resting bitch face. But that didn't deter her.

As if I summoned her, I heard her yell. "What are you doing?"

I jumped off the bed and ran towards where the sounds were coming from. Making my way down the hall to the back set of stairs, my hand at the ready on my gun.

I rushed down them, stopping dead in my tracks, seeing Anna spread open on the table.

My hand went from my gun to my cock, and neither of them noticed me standing there, gaping. I couldn't believe my eyes! The man between her legs had a tail! A fucking prehensile tail! *What the hell?*

His voice washed over my body, and my dick throbbed beneath my hand. The tailed motherfucker was Jon!

"You come when I say you do."

"Is that a fact?"

I watched as he nodded slowly. "Not a moment before."

The throbbing in my pants grew, and I rubbed along the outside, hoping for some relief.

"Jon. Please? That damn detective got me all hot and horny."

I could feel the precum oozing from my tip wetting my skin.

He stood up and leaned over her, sucking her nipple into his mouth. He let go of it and flicked his tongue across it. "I would love to see him tie you up."

She moaned and more of my cum oozed out. *Fuck! I would love to tie her up.*

"You wouldn't." She panted.

"Restrained and face-fucked."

I had to hold back my gasp when he drew blood with his bite. The combination of the scene before me and his voice making lust course through me so hard, I'm ready to fuck anything that would let me stick my cock inside.

I would grip her hair tight and pump my rod down her throat to feel her gag.

"Holding your head tight. Slamming his cock down your throat until you make him cum."

Fuck! It's like he knows what I like!

Her chest rose and fell in hard breaths. "Gonna make me swallow it all?"

"Every. Last. Drop." He leans to the other side and bites her again. "And then you'll thank him for the honor."

I couldn't take much more. I slid my hand down my pants and rubbed against my wet cock. *This should be her saliva, sucking on me begging to be fed!*

Her smokey voice came out on a husky breath. "I want to see him bend you over, hold you by your tail and fuck your ass until your nuts are bouncing together."

Never. I've never wanted to fuck a man. Until now. I couldn't close my fist around my girth. Would he be able to take my dick?

"I want to watch you both jack off and squirt all over me and then I want to be in the middle while you both fuck me." She moaned and gripped the table, panting. "I want to ride him on the couch and feel those hands gripping my hair."

Aw sweetheart, if I knew you were that kind of girl, I wouldn't have fought against my lust for you earlier.

She cried out in orgasm, locking her thighs around Jon's head.

Fuck! If she snapped his neck, that'd be so hot!

"I'd let him top!"

FUCK!

My cock exploded in my pants over my fingers, and I slowly backed up the steps. Not the easiest thing to do with your hand in your pants, but I needed to minimize the mess. Once I got to the landing, I turned and went back to my room.

That shouldn't have been so hot to watch. I shouldn't have watched it at all.

I opened the door, ducked inside and closed it fast, leaning against it. My head thumped against the wood as I tore at my pants to get them open. They hadn't even dropped to my feet before I stroked my semi-hard cock back to full hardness and rubbed a full one out.

Anna's open mouth, her soft pink tongue sticking out and licking her top lip as her chest heaved. Ass and pussy full, nipples sharply pointed up, begging for attention. Fuck! I would fill that mouth and keep her words muted, feeling her bounce between sucking me and being fucked by him.

And I gotta say, no man has ever turned me on, but seeing him naked? His thick, long cock dangling between his legs, toned body without a stitch of hair except on his head. His deep voice and those unnatural green eyes?

I could picture fucking his ass. Holding on to his tight, slim hips as he ate her pussy until she squirted on his face. That would give me a bird's eye view of her glistening pussy. She wanted to be covered in our cum and my balls had plenty backed up to give her.

My hand pistoned on my rod, squeezing tight, making the head an angry red before I released it and pumped it again. Curiosity got the better of me and I dropped to my knees. My chest heaved as I felt my climax rushing to greet me again. I stuck my middle finger in my mouth, wetting it before plunging my hand between my legs to tease my asshole.

I could feel it tighten and release as I pressed against it. Not once in my forty-some years have I wanted to feel something up my ass the way I do now. My hand choked my dick again, and I pushed my finger in slowly. It felt full and slightly uncomfortable until I rocked on my knees, fucking myself.

Moans fell softly from my mouth, intermixed with grunts of pleasure until my cock exploded all over my shirt, hitting my chin. My body froze in place as the shakes took over from the orgasm.

Slumping over, I gasped for air and felt the emptiness as I pulled my finger out.

"Jesus, Dom!" I panted and rolled to my side, feeling better than I had in weeks.

There were two quick knocks on the door, and then I heard Jon. "Dinner's in an hour, Detective. Do you need anything?"

My hand grabbed my chest, worried that he'd open the door. "No."

"Are you sure?" He chuckled.

My heart slowed, and I shook my head. *There's no way he knows what I was doing.* "Actually, since I'm stuck here overnight, could you grab my bag from the trunk of my car? It has my spare clothing in it."

"Absolutely. Is it locked?"

"Yeah." I blew out a breath. "Keys are in my blazer pocket."

"I'll have that right in."

"Good deal. I'm going to shower, so you can leave it on the bed."

Straining my ears, I listened for his footfalls and once I knew he had walked away; I got up, stripped my clothes, tossed them in a pile, and strolled naked to the shower. Turning it on, I set the temp as hot as it would go, then stepped in and let the water rinse away all traces of what I'd done.

I heard the door open and then heard it close again as I stood under the hot water. The man wasn't anything if not efficient. Grabbing the small soap, I opened it and lathered my body. The scent reminded me of a coffee shop, and my skin felt entirely too clean after using it.

Laughing to myself in the small space, I spoke to the water, "squeaky clean!"

Next I reached for the shampoo and took care of my hair, then I rinsed off and got out, wrapping a towel around my waist. As I stepped from the bathroom, I saw my bag on the bed and on the small table a tray sat with a drink.

Walking over, I lifted the glass, and the aromatic smell of whiskey permeated my nose. A note sat on the tray.

You strike me as a whiskey man.

Enjoy,

A

A smile cracked my face. "Good call." I lifted the drink in the air in a toast and slammed the drink down, savoring the smooth, rich, nutty flavor. My chest felt warm as the liquid made its way through my body. "Not only a good call, but an excellent whiskey to boot."

I turned to my bag, opened it and pulled out jeans and a tee. I usually kept this in my car as a backup because one too many times my work clothes got fucked up.

Taking the tray and the glass, I left my room and went back to the kitchen. Instead of running this time, I walked and took in the décor. The Serene Raven had some amazing antiques, and I realized I felt relaxed.

When was the last time I felt this relaxed?

That thought troubled me. I couldn't think of the last time I truly relaxed and enjoyed being somewhere. As I walked down the stairs, I heard Anna singing. Even her singing voice enchanted me.

She stood over the stove stirring something, her hips gracefully moving as her skirt swished at her knees.

"Hello, Detective." She glanced over her shoulder at me. "Did you rest well?"

"I did." I set the tray on the side of the sink with the glass. "That smells delicious."

She turned and faced me, wiping her hands on her apron. "I'm a fabulous cook." She winked and stepped closer. "Mm. You tried my soap."

With her close, my jeans got tighter. "I'm squeaky clean."

"That's a good thing."

I stared at her full lips, painted red, slightly parted that looked like they were made for kissing. They also made me think of her on her knees, sucking my dick with my fist in her hair as she gasped for breath. My cock throbbed in my jeans, and I fought the urge to reach out and push her down to the floor.

Her sultry voice broke through my thoughts. "You know, it would be nice if I could call you something other than detective."

"Dom." My voice came out low and husky. "It's short for Dominick."

"Well. *Dom*." Her tongue poked out and licked her lower lip. "Where would you like to eat?"

I glanced at the kitchen table and the vision of her on her back, legs open, popped into my head. "Right here looks good enough to me."

She batted her blue eyes, and Jon's voice came from behind me. "Here you go, Detective." He pulled the chair out. "Your seat is ready."

"You, uh, can call me Dom."

"Dom." His voice purred. "Would you like another drink?"

"Please." I nodded over my shoulder and then turned to take my seat.

Anna spun on her toes and went back to the stove. Her movements were graceful as she reached for plates and filled them. She served me first, and then set a place for Jon and finally made her own plate.

She sat across the table from me, and when Jon came back, he sat at the head of the table and set my drink down by my plate. We all tucked into our plates and my first bite of the steak melted in my mouth.

"This is amazing!" A small moan followed my words.

"Thank you." Her smile felt like a shot to my heart. A woman who liked dirty sex, talked dirty and could cook like a Michelin star chef. She felt too good to be true. "Tell me, Dom, how is a handsome man like you still unattached?"

I chuffed out a laugh. "Just lucky I guess." My right shoulder lifted in a shrug. "Long hours don't sit well with most women."

"Fools." Jon shook his head.

We ate in companionable silence, and when we were done, Anna cleared the dishes. "You look tired. I bet a good night of sleep will do you wonders."

"Storms like this are good sleeping weather." Jon winked.

Tilting my head, I looked over at him. *What is he?* Right now he looked human, no sign of the tail I saw earlier. *Maybe you were hallucinating?*

"Good idea." I pushed back from the table. "Thank you. Your hospitality is a welcome change."

Anna stepped closer to me and wrapped her arms around my neck, pressing her body against mine. My arms wrapped around her in return, and I felt her lips brush against my neck. "Sleep sweet, Dom."

A shiver ran through my body and the overwhelming urge to sweep her up in my arms and take her to bed with me made it difficult to step back. I'm not sure how long we stood there, but it must've been longer than I thought when I heard Jon speak.

"A nightcap for you, sir." He held out a fresh drink.

I released Anna and accepted the drink as I left the kitchen and went back to my room.

Anna

The jeans Dom wore only highlighted his ass better than the slacks from earlier. My tongue ran along the bottoms of my teeth as I pictured biting into it and tasting his sweet blood.

Jon stood behind me and wrapped his arms around my waist. “You know, he saw us earlier.”

“Good.”

He leaned closer to my ear. “Do you wish to hold off on tonight’s playtime?”

Laughter bubbled up from my chest. “Don’t be absurd. The moon is full. She’s ready and you know I don’t miss my beauty treatments.”

“You should rest for tonight.” His forked tongue tickled my ear. “Go on.”

I turned in his arms and brushed my lips against his. “I can’t wait for you to wake me.”

Leaving his embrace, I strolled to my room and stripped down naked. I crawled under the covers on my bed and, hugging my pillow close, I drifted into a meditative state. Memories filled my head as I lay there.

I still relish the look of horror in my parents' eyes as I knelt on the bed by them with my athame and cut their tongues out. The feel of their warm, sticky blood covering my hands. Such power! I was in control and here it is thirty years later and no one is the wiser.

Detective Moody and his entire department can go over the evidence all they want. They'll find nothing. Here in Castle Hollow, the darkness is in everyone. People who rave about Mister Graves restaurant have no idea that most of the meat is long pig.

I could feel the smile on my lips thinking of the reincarnated village leader and his taste for human meat. And our church? Abbott Jesus Chavez had a cult following, believing he was the true son of God sent to redeem us all.

And Sheriff Hugh Lincoln? That man had a hair trigger and most of the criminals met their demise at the end of his loaded gun.

Magic purred in the air. I wasn't the only witch and most of the town knew who they were in past lives. We made no excuse for who we were. Why would we? With safety in numbers, we took care of our own.

Rolling to my back, a vision pushed its way to the front. I looked down at the young girl beneath me and saw hands around her slender throat. I felt them tightening as though they were my hands. As she gasped for air, I watched in lustful excitement. A thin sheen of sweat covered her skin and she let out a soft moan.

"That's it, moan for me." Dominick's guttural voice growled, and he thrust his hips into her harder.

My body wasn't mine. To be seeing this means the concoction I mixed up for Dominick worked. This was *his* memory. I rode his emotions and felt each pump of his hips fucking her hard. Her sweet pussy tightening around his thick cock and he tightened his hands in one last squeeze.

"Moan, bitch." He panted and trembled when her weak moan wheezed out.

His groans filled the room, rasping grunts. as he panted and exploded inside her. His hands loosened as he pushed off from her neck, rolling to the side to catch his breath.

My naughty detective didn't look back as he rolled from the bed and went to shower. Excitement still running in his veins, he jacked off in the shower, replaying the scene in his head as both piss and cum oozed out of his dick.

Stepping from the bathroom, the whore he fucked hadn't moved from the bed. He stepped closer and gave her a nudge. When she didn't respond, he reached down to check for a pulse, and found nothing.

He ran his hand through his thick, wet hair. "Shit."

He walked around the bed and grabbed his phone.

"I got another one for you."

A laugh came from the other side. "Again? Damn, brother."

"Yeah, well. I'll meet you at the farm." He disconnected the call and tossed his phone on the bed, then he got dressed and then dressed her.

He carried her out to his car, and set her in as though she slept deeply.

Dom cranked the radio up and sang along, his thumbs drumming against the steering wheel as he drove to a farm two cities over.

My sweet man didn't break a sweat, nor did he worry.

When he arrived at the farm, a young man who looked similar to him came to the car.

"Gonna pay me?" The younger one winked.

Dom handed him a wad of cash and motioned to the passenger seat with his head. The younger man stuffed the money in his pocket and went around the car and took the dead hooker out, tossing her over his shoulder, and headed towards the barn.

He gave a wave behind him and called out. "The pigs thank you for the treat, Dom."

A loud clap of thunder pulled me from my dreams and I sat up, looking around my room. My eyes landed on my clock and I smiled. Jon would come up to wake me soon and Ollin Graves would be here to collect fresh meat for the restaurant.

Lightning flashed and illuminated my perfect skin, still firm and youthful at forty-three. My bedroom door opened and my lover walked in.

"That doesn't look like a nap." Jon's eyebrow raised.

"The potion worked." I bounced up to my knees. "He's one of us."

Jon's eyes flashed with lust. "What's his poison?"

My head fell back in laughter. "Hookers."

He bent over laughing with me and then came closer, holding out his hand. "Come, my love. Ollin is here waiting."

I slipped my tiny hand into his and let him pull me close. His lips brushed against mine, and his forked tongue plunged forcefully into my mouth. Our tongues battled for dominance as his hands caressed my body.

His claws capered down my back and I grabbed his head, holding him to me as we kissed. Once I felt his hands cup my ass, I jumped up and wrapped my legs around his waist, grinding my wet, fiery core against his covered erection.

He carried me from my room through the halls and down to the kitchen. My hips pumped against him, reveling in the friction on my clit. Without breaking our kiss, he carried me down the private stairs that lead to the dungeon.

This specially built area had mirrors around the walls, five chaise loungers around the walls and windows that welcomed the moonlight when the drapes were drawn, and a small table of tools. I broke the kiss and, grasping his shoulders, rode against him harder and felt my orgasm rolling through me, soaking his pants.

"Mm. Oh, oh, oh!" I tightened my legs around him and lifted my head to see the young naked young girl dangling from her chains in the moonlight, waiting to be sacrificed.

Jon waited for my legs to unlock before he helped me to my feet. He took a seat beside Ollin. Not only did he love fresh meat, but he loved to jack off watching me get my sacrifice ready. I looked around and saw the sheriff on a chaise of his own.

"Welcome, Hugh." My steps were seductive as I crossed the room to him. "What can I do for you?"

His hand rubbed his erection outside his pants and his dark eyes looked into mine, then down to his lap.

"That's right." I smiled and turned to the young girl. "You promised the sheriff here a blow job if he wouldn't arrest you."

Her head bobbed in the affirmative and I gave Hugh a cheeky wink and walked to the girl. "Are you ready to play?"

She blinked her innocent eyes at me, and I reached for the key to undo the lock. I grabbed her face in my hand and squeezed it hard, watching her saliva ooze around the gag. "Be a good girl and I'll take the gag out."

Her eyes widened, and she bobbed her head the best she could in my grip. My tongue licked the side of her face over to her ear. "You taste so sweet."

Reaching around her head, I undid the ball gag and removed it from her mouth. She stretched her jaw and moved it all around before looking at me through her eyelashes. "Thank you, Mistress."

"Aw, baby knows her place." The back of my hand skimmed along her cheek. "Good girl."

"I...I... puh... please?"

"Please what?"

She blinked her eyes at me, and her mouth fell open like a fresh-caught fish. Blowing out a nervous breath, I set the key back down and then reached for her breasts, latching onto her nipples with my fingers.

"Mistress, please?" Her bottom lip trembled, and I took my hold on her nipples from holding on to a hard grip, making her gasp in pain. "Mmmmm." She moaned and shook.

"Sheriff Lincoln has been waiting for your mouth to suck his dick." I twisted her nipples. "Are you ready to fulfill your offer?"

"Yes!" she cried out in a moan.

Releasing her nipples, they turn bright red as the blood rushes back to them. She trembles, pressing her legs together. I reach for the key and make fast work of the lock. Her arms fall as gravity takes hold, yanking them down.

She cried out in pain again and fell to her knees. I reached for my riding crop on my work table and slapped her ass hard. "Get going. That dick ain't gonna suck itself!" I brought the crop down again as she made her first motion.

Hugh's face lit up, and he opened his pants, letting his cock spring out. A nice long skinny one, perfect to feed down someone's throat.

"Take your pants down more, Hugh." I snap her ass again. "I know how much you like your asshole tongued."

"Smack her again. Make that ass tender." Ollin licks his lips. "You know how I like my meat."

I bring the crop down harder, peppering swats all over her ass, legs, and ribs, making her dance on her hands and knees.

Hugh gets comfy on the chaise, spreading his legs wide. "Show me what a good girl you are." His voice is ominous as he holds his cock out for her mouth.

I drop to my knees behind her, grab a fistful of hair and yank her head back, swatting at her tits with the crop. "Thank him for your gift."

"Th... th.. thank you." She panted, and her tongue stuck out for him to place his cock on.

"Yeah, swirl your tongue around the head." He moaned. "Push it inside the piss slit."

I held my hand out for my athame, and Jon placed it in my hand, kneeling behind me. "What will it be? My cock in your ass? Or shall I suck off Ollin?"

"Mm, suck his cock." I rubbed my hard nipples against my sacrifice's back. "Ou skondro ousmei ou, cre skondro ousmei cre!" Thunder clapped and lightning flashed as I yelled out my spell and smiled. *Let's see how dirty Dom really is. Enjoy the show, Detective.*

I handed Hugh the crop and wrapped my arm around the girl in my arms. My fingers found her nipples puckered tight, and I flicked at each one, going back and forth between them. My body shifted and moved closer to Hugh. I felt his hand push mine aside.

Turning my head, I saw Jon deep throat Ollin making the older man's eyes roll to the back of his head. He gave a satisfied sigh and then turned his attention to us.

"Pinch those tits. Keep them tender." Ollin growled.

"Hear that? Chef wants them tender." I purred in her ear and pinched the skin and fat all around her tits, pulling on her nipples while Hugh shoved his cock down her throat, making her audibly gag.

My right hand slid down her body, pausing for small pinches until I reached her wet pussy. I rubbed my fingers in the wetness and brought my hand back to my face for a taste. Tonight's sacrifice loved being used for sex. The wetness came from her cunt. Not a drop of pee mixed in.

"If you want, I can lick your pussy." I nipped her ear. "All you need to do is let me between your legs."

She immediately sat up higher and I moved onto my back and slid between them. She smelled so sweet and musky. My tongue flattened and pushed between her lips with my nose, bumping her clit. Her hips moved on my face and I reached up to pull on her nipples again. Each pull granted me a small gush of her cream.

"That's it, come on her face!" Hugh yelled.

Moans from Ollin and Hugh filled the room, and my pussy ached. I needed something to fuck it. *Anything* would do. A tongue, finger, dick, the handle of the crop. My lips locked on to her clit and I bit it over and over until I tasted blood and felt juice flow from me onto the floor.

"Yeah! You like my balls bouncing on your chin!" Hugh groaned. "Fuck! I don't know where I want to cum. Down your pretty throat all over your body."

"Wherever you want, sir." She cried out, and I almost drowned in the flood of her orgasm.

I pushed out from between her legs and saw Dom standing at the foot of the stairs in his boxers. His eyes were wide and his mouth opened in disbelief.

"Your tits win." Hugh growled and grunted his release all over her. "Evening, Detective."

Dominick

A loud thunderclap pulled me from sleep, and as I re-closed my eyes, I saw the debauchery unfolding. My dick hardened, and I looked around in my vision to see where they were. Slipping out from the covers, I left my room and felt a pull toward the kitchen.

Following my gut, I turned and walked down the hall briskly, jogging down the steps into the dark kitchen. My head spun on my shoulders, investigating the walls as I walked toward the back door. With my hand on the knob, I felt a whisper to my right. It felt like an invitation, and I slowly turned to where it came from. Looking at the bare wall, my hand left the knob and settled against the cool satin surface, feeling around.

Like a blind person, I felt my way all over and then gave the wall a push and a door popped open.

Voices, moans and the sweet scent of sex hit me. I felt like a kid finding his dad's porn stash and filled with excitement. My bare feet hit the steps as the door closed behind me. I ran down the stairs like a kid on Christmas morning and no one noticed me standing there in my boxers as I watched Sheriff Lincoln blow his load all over a young woman. Anna sat up on her side, her face shimmering in cum.

“Your tits win.” He grunted as he covered her in cum. “Evening, Detective.” he growled.

“Is the party over?” My hoarse voice croaked out.

My cock tented my boxers and bobbed, wanting attention, and I wanted to join in the scene before me. This was something I craved. Dark, delicious, dirty sex where your fantasies came to life.

Sheriff Lincoln stroked his softening cock and tilted his head, looking at me. “Depends.”

Jon pulled back from the man he was sucking off and smiled at me. “Our good detective here has the darkness inside him.”

“Is your tongue forked?” I leaned in closer.

“Yessss.” He hissed. “Better to pleasure you with.”

The man Jon pulled from motioned with his finger to the girl and she crawled to him, taking his cock in her mouth. “Whew. Hugh, you got her all warmed up.”

Jon crawled closer to me and nuzzled my cock. “Let me show you.” His forked tongue snaked out and into the hole in my boxers. It tickled the underside and then wrapped around me, coaxing my erection out through the hole.

A growl rumbled up from my chest as I watched Anna play with her breasts. “Turn so I can see that beautiful pussy of yours.”

Her eyes darkened in lust and she shifted her position and spread her legs wide open the way she had on the table earlier. "Like what you see?"

My hand petted Jon's head as I kept my eyes on her. "Stop teasing me and suck it."

His tongue unwound from my cock and slithered inside my boxers again, this time finding my asshole and teasing me before tickling my taint and my balls. He leaned his head back and licked up my length.

"Finger that cunt." I glowered at Anna. "I want to see how wet you get."

My head fell back when Jon closed his mouth around my head. He sucked hard and fed my length down his throat. Without thinking, my hands moved to his throat and my thumbs massaged just above his Adam's apple.

Off to the side, the sheriff stroked his cock, which stood hard and ready for more action. The girl had her face buried against the old man's nest of hair.

Sharp, talon-like claws dug into my hips, and they ripped my boxers from my body. Jon winked at me while he bobbed on my dick and I watched his tail sway in the air. Hugh's gruff voice broke my concentration.

"Get up on this dick, Anna."

She blew a kiss my way and crawled over to him. I watched as she stood up, turned around to face me, and then crouched as he fed his cock into her wet hole. He fucked her slowly, his hands cupping her breasts and teasing her nipples.

My eyes narrowed with pleasure, and I longed to take control of the room. With a nod at Anna, I asked the sheriff. “How's her pussy feel, Lincoln?”

He let out a long, low moan and thrust his hips up, making her tits bounce. “How'd'ya think it feels?”

Anna licked her fingers and stroked them on her nipples. “My pussy is silk.”

“I'll find out later.” I growled at her.

“Of that I have no doubt.” She rolled her hips and moaned.

Jon sucked on my head, using his tongue to tease me, then took me all the way down his throat so my thumbs could feel the tip. He repeated the action a few times, and I fought against blowing my load down his throat.

The old man screamed and went into what looked like an epileptic seizure as he came down her throat. She took it all and lapped at his head before taking him into her mouth to clean him up. When she finished, she sat back on her heels and he patted his lap. She moved to lie over it and he spanked her. Each swat echoed louder than the one before it as he paddled her ass harder with each swat, alternating cheeks.

“I can't wait to take you home, sweetie.” He smiled and rubbed her sore ass.

Hugh chuckled. “I think he's almost done playing with his food.”

“Mm.” Anna moaned. “I know I'm ready for more.”

“Hey Ollin, let's get her set up.” Hugh pushed Anna up and off his cock, then met the old man in the middle of the room.

I finally took a moment to look around at my surroundings. There were a multitude of mirrors so everyone could see their actions, lounges to sit or lie on for sex, and enough moonlight streaming in to add to the atmosphere.

I tightened my grip on Jon's throat. "Like that?"

He growled and his teeth scraped my sensitive skin, making me shiver. His green eyes glimmered as he pulled his head back. He pushed his skinny fork down my slit. My ass cheeks tightened, and I let out a guttural scream.

"Fuck!" I blasted the back of Jon's throat with cum. Pump after pump, he swallowed it all down while I glued my eyes on the scene before me. I pulled my cock from Jon's mouth, still hard. My hand reached down, stroking it while Jon moved behind the woman, wrapping his tail around her middle.

Anna bent over lewdly, exposing her juicy pussy to me as she picked up a knife from the floor. The two men held the young woman's arms out between them, and Jon's leg pushed between hers. His hand cupped her mound, his fingers deep inside her core. Her head rolled back to rest on his shoulder while she enjoyed the finger fucking.

"Your time has come. The purpose for which you were born for is here." She leaned in and kissed the girl and then trailed kisses around her breasts, licking the dried cum from them. I stepped closer and felt electricity in the air. The hair on my arms and legs danced in the currents as I reached out to touch Anna.

"Mm, Dom, come closer." Her free hand reached for me and I stepped up, pulling her naked body against mine, rubbing my cock between her ass cheeks.

She lifted her arms up and wrapped them around my neck, lifting her tits up. She wiggled her hips to play with my dick and her head tilted back as her sultry voice filled the room. "Rojhugbroie eleigoaiwaie zaiii oa ecr bloawawuo zaiii awogl'gsc! Afeiwuie mob wafie fribranfaipgroidgro scec ecr eijo scec jou!"

Thunder and lightning went nuts and Anna let go of my neck and reached for her knife, bringing it to the girl's throat and sliced from ear to ear. She slid down my body, falling to her knees, and pulled the knife down the center of the woman's body, letting the blood rain all over her.

From her hair to her feet, blood covered her. She dropped the knife and rubbed it over her arms, stomach, and breasts. I may not have seen a sacrifice before, but I knew what I had become part of. The older men held the woman until she took her last breath and then carried her from the room.

Anna spun her body around and her bloody hands closed around my dick, stroking me. The warm blood felt like heaven, and then she licked my head and sucked it into her mouth, making me hiss.

Little did she know of my bloodlust, but it appeared she had it as well. She rose to her knees and wrapped her mouth around me, not able to take me as deep as Jon did. That didn't matter though. Her hot mouth sucking me made my toes curl.

Her bloody hands rubbed my body in the still warm liquid and I reached down to pull her up. She batted her eyes at me and leaned in to lick my lips. A loud growl came from somewhere deep inside me as I tasted the blood.

I should be disgusted. I should call this in, but I'm not. Right now, all I wanted was to bury my cock in her silken pussy and make her cry out my name.

As I reached for her, I slammed my lips against hers. She opened her mouth, letting me in, as I lifted her by her ass. She knew what I wanted, and she jumped up, wrapping her legs around me. I walked us to the nearest wall and lined my cock up with her hole.

"Fuck me." Her voice came out breathy as she shifted, trying to be filled.

My hips thrust up, and my hand went around her throat. "Is my cock better than his tail?"

Jon's dick rubbed against my ass crack. "Does your ego need stroking?"

"I just don't want to compete with whatever the fuck you are." My heart raced in my chest. *Her pussy really is silk.*

"You did see us." She moaned and smiled at Jon. "So much thicker." She panted.

"Incubus." He hissed in my ear.

"My sexy sex demon." She said at the same time and her pussy clenched my dick.

I tightened my hand on her throat. "She was one of the missing girls."

Her voice softened with the lack of oxygen. "Oops."

I thrust harder inside of her. Her pussy fit around my cock like a glove, and I couldn't relax my hold on her throat. The wall behind her cracked from the force of our three bodies and her eyes widened with a wheezing moan.

"You know you want to feel his tail." She licked at my lips and then bit the bottom one.

With a snarl, I shoved her back on the wall and I felt something poking at my tight hole.

"Just a taste." Jon purred and peppered kisses on my shoulders. "Feel the soft tip, teasing you."

My breathing hitched, and I felt a pop of pain. "That's a good boy. Let me make you feel good."

His tail throbbed and teased my stretched hole as I fucked Anna. His hands played between us, pinching our nipples together, and I felt the orgasm of a lifetime building in my body.

"Dom!" Her soft voice tickled my ears. "Oh, Dom!" I felt her pussy milk my cock. And I let my hand loosen around her throat. Jon pushed his tail in further and my body shook from my toes to my hair.

"Anna!" I cried out and came inside her, holding us where we were while we calmed down. Hands flittered and caressed my body, and I dropped my head to meet hers. "So fucking good."

"My sweet dark detective." She softly purred.

"Our." Jon corrected her, and his claws traced my ribs on my side. "Deviant." He bit my neck and my body twitched.

"Our sweet, dark, deviant detective." Her tongue poked out and licked at my lips. "Kiss me."

I crashed my lips against hers in a hungry kiss. I wanted more, but I felt my cock softening inside her.

Jon pressed tender kisses into my shoulders and neck while his claws continued to tease my skin. My cock slipped from her wet pussy and I wasn't sure I remembered how to breathe. The room spun around me. Soon, blackness followed, seeping in from the edges of my sight until I fell into oblivion.

Dominick

The sound of an old phone ringing woke me. My eyes fluttered open, and light filtered through a haze, almost blinding me. Each ring of the phone pounded inside my head as though I had tiny gnomes cobbling shoes in there.

With a groan, I rolled towards the sound and slammed my hand down in search of the torture device. My fingers finally found the handset, and I fumbled, lifting it off the cradle.

Who the fuck has landlines anymore?

The ringing started back up and I threw myself in the general direction to pick it up, this time growling into the receiver. "Someone better be dead."

"Well, since you're not at work, I worried you might be." My partner's smooth voice filled my ear.

"It's the middle of the night."

He chuffed in my ear. "Try noon."

I patted the surface with my hands and determined I was in bed. After blinking a few more times, I opened my eyes fully and looked at my surroundings while still laying in the bed.

The antique furniture, heavy drapes and cloud-like bed told me I woke up in the Serene Raven. The clock by the side of the bed confirmed the time. My hand scrubbed over my face, and I shook my head.

What the hell happened last night?

"Man, I feel like I just went to bed."

This time, he laughed. "What the hell did you do? Tie one on to celebrate the rain?"

I remember eating dinner with Anna and Jon, then I came back to my room and crawled into bed to do some reading on my phone.

"Why didn't my alarm go off?" Sitting up, I looked for my phone and found it under a pillow.

Checking the phone log, I saw the alarm sounded and I must've shut it off, along with several missed calls from Sean. I flopped back on the bed and covered my eyes with my arm. Nothing felt real right now. As a matter of fact, it all felt very surreal. There's no way I could have fallen asleep last night, then woken up for a sex party and sacrifice of a woman... Wait. She felt familiar. Where have I seen her before?

My arm bounced on my head as I mentally flipped through images in my mind.

"Holy shit!" I sat up, slapping my head. "One of the missing girls was there!"

"Where?"

"Here!" Jumping out of the bed, I held my arms out and searched my body, and there wasn't one speck of blood. I remembered a demon cutting my boxers from my body, but here I stood wearing intact boxers.

"What the fuck is going on?" I yelled into both the room and phone, hoping for an answer. *Any* answer.

"Moody! What the hell?"

That wasn't the answer I had been hoping for.

"I... I... don't know. Was I fucking dreaming?"

"That's it. I'm coming to you. Hold tight, brother." He hung up, and I stood there, still looking at my boxers in awe.

I grabbed my bag and went through it, not even sure what to be looking for. My head swiveled, looking around the room. Something in the air felt off. After replacing the handset in the cradle, I grabbed my jeans from the chair and slid them on along with my tee, and left my room to solve my personal mystery before Sean arrived.

Anna

Moisture hung in the air, making my limbs feel heavier than they were. I used my arm to brush my bangs back and continued working on the yard. Storms like the one last night wreak havoc on trees, flowers, and anything else in their way.

On the flip side, the grass seemed greener, many things sprouted taller, and the sun marked the beginning of a new day. I could respect a fabulous storm like last night. The moon glowed in the sky, highlighting the storm's fierce anger. It set the tone for my ritual and in the end, just as the storm did some damage to the outside, I did a little inside and my skin tightened, any little wrinkles worked themselves out and there was not a gray hair on my head.

I slept gloriously, too. Dom not only had a big dick, that man knew how to use it. The best part lay in knowing he liked it as rough and animalistic as I did. Glancing over my shoulder, I caught sight of the cut from the broken mirror sliding into me while he fucked me up against the wall.

This scar I planned to keep.

Jon cleaned up after the party and I don't mean just the room. I mean everything. Me. The room. And Dom. He even put the good detective to bed.

I continued picking up the small branches and debris that covered the lawn while I let myself remember Dom's handsome face. A soft moan escaped my lips. The way his blue eyes lit up seeing us all. It excited him the way it does me. The way it does everyone who belonged in Castle Hollow.

I've been up since the sun broke on the horizon, which gave me plenty of time to have a chat with sheriff Lincoln. Turns out there's been more than one woman of the night who went missing and he smiled when I told him I might know something about that.

Seeing my deviant detective choke a girl and cart her off to a pig farm made me wet. I can't wait to share that with him. He wasn't repulsed by my ritual. He loved the feel of my warm bloody hands touching him.

Yes. I think he belongs here in Castle Hollow with the rest of us, where we can live in peace.

A light blue sedan pulled into the driveway and I watched an older man park and exit the vehicle. He gave me a wave as he walked toward me. "Good afternoon, ma'am."

"Afternoon." I wiped my forehead with my arm. "What can I do for you?"

"I'm detective Sean Riley and I'm looking for my partner." His voice was scratchy and his face had worry lines creasing on his forehead.

"Detective Moody was still resting, last I knew." I smiled and pulled my garden gloves off. "Let's go inside where you can check on him and I can get you something to drink."

They must be close for him to drive out here and check on Dom. It never occurred to me he had to check in anywhere or be some place else.

"Thank you." He motioned for me to go first and I appeased him by going up the steps as he instructed, then I held the door for him to enter the inn.

"I guess it's my turn to thank you." He chuckled as he crossed the threshold.

"If we keep this up, we'll get nowhere except a circle of politeness." I followed him in and closed the door. "I'm Anna Bishop and this is my inn."

He stood there stoically and said nothing as I turned away from him. My eyes rolled in my head. I hated when people didn't respond to what I'd said and I led him to the kitchen. I motioned to the table, and he took the hint by sitting down.

"What can I get you to drink?" I asked, while washing my hands in the sink.

He cleared his throat. "I'd like to see detective Moody first."

"Of course." I reached for the towel and turned, smiling at him. "I'll go get him."

After leaving the room, I made my way up the stairs to the hallway where his room was located. Taking my time, I strolled up the landing and walked down the hall until I reached room thirteen and gave the door two sharp knocks.

When there was no answer, I knocked again and opened the door to peer inside. The empty, disheveled bed told me he'd awaken. I went all the way in and checked the bathroom, to no avail. My deviant must've gone exploring.

Dominick

Before Sean arrived, I made a trip to the secret basement and felt even more confused. The mirrors I remembered around the room weren't there, there wasn't a hook to hang someone up in the middle of the room and the chaise loungers where I thought I saw the sheriff and the other old man were missing.

There were no peculiar smells, only the smell of mothballs and a hint of something flowery. No broken glass from where I thought I fucked Anna against the wall. There wasn't a speck of blood to be found. Everything looked spotless. Gazing around, all I saw were boxes that held old books, knickknacks, and extra hotel supplies. There were even boxes of ingredients for Anna's boutique.

"What the fuck is going on?" My voice bounced off the boxes, but none of them answered me.

After walking around for a second time, I gave up and went back up the stairs and back to my room. I paced, trying to recount what happened last night. I remembered dinner, nothing out of the ordinary. Then I had a nightcap and kicked back in bed.

I don't remember when I fell asleep, but I know a loud clap of thunder woke me. I had been dreaming about a small sex party featuring Anna and another woman. Maybe that was all it was. Simply a dream?

My stomach grumbled loudly, and I knew I needed some food, so I made my way to the kitchen and found Sean sitting there.

Why is he here?

"Dom!" He stood up and came over. "Are you okay?"

The phone call. I must've sounded like a drunkard.

"I don't know what I am right now." My hand came up and rubbed my furrowed brows. "I think maybe I was wrong. It was a dream"

"Wrong about?" he pulled me towards the table.

I took a seat and waited for him to do the same before I looked him in the eyes. "About seeing that girl." Looking around the kitchen, I didn't see Anna. "Where's Anna?"

"Anna?" He looked at me, confused. "OH! You mean the owner?"

"Yeah." I nodded and got up to look down the hall into the front room.

"Dom. Sit down. I need you to make sense." The firmness in his voice told me he might lose his temper soon.

I went back to the table. "Where did you see her?"

"She was cleaning up the lawn outside, escorted me in and then went looking for you." His nostrils flared. "So did you, or didn't you, see her?" He held his hands out frustratedly.

"No, I haven't seen her." I shook my head.

"Concentrate. Dominick." He growled. "I'm not talking about fucking Anna."

"What?" I sat back in the chair. "Who are you talking about?"

"The missing girl you think you saw."

With a shake of my head, I looked at him. "I don't know."

"What do you *mean*, you don't know?" He grabbed my arms to get my full attention. "You're still not making any sense."

"I think it was a dream." I nodded.

He growled at me and his fingers dug into my skin. "What was a dream?"

My chest puffed up, and I chuckled. "I had the most vivid dream of my life." I sat back, blowing out a hard breath. "I thought I saw the missing girl here." All around me, I motioned. "But I was wrong."

"You've said that. Three times now. *Where in this place* did you see her?" My partner leaned in closer.

I shook my head. "I don't know. I just remember a room of people."

"What are you not saying, Dom?" My partner's voice sounded frustrated, and I didn't blame him. I sounded like a loon.

Sean lifted his head and his tone changed when he spoke to her. "Hello Miss Anna."

"I see you found him." She smiled and walked closer. "Can I get either of you a drink? Dom? Would you like some brunch?"

Her dark eyes peered into mine and I felt less confused. I let out a soft sigh and shook my head again. "You know what I would like?"

"Hm, if this is a game where I guess I'll guess you're a pancake man." She gave me a cheeky wink.

A small smile spread across my face. "That sounds great. Coffee too?"

"Anything you'd like." She walked over and slipped her apron over her clothes. "It'll be ready before you know it. Would you like some as well, detective?"

She glanced over her shoulder and I caught her watching him scratch his stubbled face. "Sure. What the hell."

"What the hell, indeed." She laughed and got busy cooking.

I sat there staring at the table, listening to her walk around, the clangs of the griddle being put on the stove and her mixing the batter while still mulling over the events in my mind.

What I really remembered wasn't something you shared with someone you work with. There's no way that the sex I had last night was a dream.

I tasted her. I felt her heartbeat against my fingers when they were wrapped around her pretty little throat. The way her pussy fit around my cock. I remember her fucking the sheriff and Jon tempting me when I let him suck me off.

Last night's dream came true. I could be myself and enjoy sex. No. It wasn't a dream. But being part of a ritual where a young woman was drained of her blood. I'm in it now. If I admit what I saw, then I have to admit to being a part of it.

And that's something I'm not ready to do.

Anna

I heard part of their conversation and couldn't help but wonder if we were wrong about Dom. He claimed he saw the girl, but then said it had to be a dream. Perhaps a conversation between him and the sheriff needed to take place.

I finished mixing my pancake batter, and while waiting for the griddle to heat, I served them coffee. Detective Sean Riley kept his eyes on me and every move I made. I'm not sure what he thought he would see. I'm used to people staring at me because of my beauty, but this felt different.

He didn't trust me.

The batter sizzled as I poured it onto the griddle and I focused my attention on the pancakes. Sean's grizzled voice made the hairs on my neck stand on end.

"Miss Anna, I know my partner showed you some pictures yesterday. Would you take another look for me today?"

"Of course, detective." I tossed over my shoulder. "Just let me finish cooking."

A snarl curled on my lips. *What does he think I'll say? Oh yes, she helped me with my beauty routine?*

Dom cleared his throat. "I already showed her all the photos, Sean."

"I know. But maybe without the distraction of a storm, she'll remember something."

A loud laugh bubbled up from me. "Please, storms haven't bothered me my whole life. I adore a magnificent storm."

I loaded up the plates and served the men at my table. Before I sat down, I got them syrup, butter and utensils, then got myself a cup of tea.

With a motion of my hand, I caught Sean's eyes. "May I see the photos?

He reached into his jacket pocket and pulled out the photos, handing them to me. I took my time with each of the four pictures.

I recognized each of the girls, but I didn't tell Dom, and I sure as hell wasn't going to tell Sean. What happened in Castle Hollow stayed in Castle Hollow. We were tighter lipped than cheating spouses who went to Vegas.

"No, detective." I looked up at him. "I've not seen any of these girls."

"I'm curious. If they had passed through Castle Hollow, where would be a location they might stop?"

"Well. There's the diner. The Salty Chef." I smiled. "Or Raven's convenience store. Saint Vincent's church and the Order of the Vine monastery pulled in visitors. We have a waterfall hidden in the forest by the mountains.

Maybe the grocery store?" My right shoulder lifted in a small shrug.

Sean pulled out a small notepad and scribbled notes from what I told him.

"The storm was too bad last night for me to talk with anyone at those locations." Dom took a drink of his coffee and sat there quietly. "I don't remember talking to the sheriff here." He looked at his partner. "Do you?"

"No. We should do that too." He took another bite of pancake. "Divide and conquer? Or together?"

I hated the feeling that Dom would leave the inn so soon; I needed to distract him to keep him here with me. Even if it's for a short time. The sexy detective captivated my interest, and I wanted to fuck him one more time. Letting my shoe slide off my foot quietly, I teased Dom's leg with my toes.

He closed his eyes for a moment, appearing deep in thought, and I felt his hands grab my foot, guiding it to feel his erection. When he opened his eyes, he whispered. "Divide and conquer."

Sean looked over at me, and his eyes narrowed a hair. "Thank you for your hospitality."

Tsk-tsk, Sean, pussy trumps work.

"You're welcome." I pulled my foot away from Dom and slipped my shoe back on. "May I take your plate?"

"Sure."

I stood up and felt Dom's eyes on me this time. It wasn't the same distrustful gaze as his partner. Dom had lust in his eyes, and I felt him zero in on my ass.

It confirmed my assumptions when Sean snapped his fingers to get Dom's attention.

"Man, I just asked you where you plan to start." Irritation laced his voice.

"Sorry. I think I'm still groggy from last night." Dom's husky voice caused goose bumps on my skin, because I knew the truth. "I'll start with the sheriff."

"That'll work. Just text me who you're going to talk to next, and I'll do the same." Sean's chair scraped the floor. "I'll meet up with you later."

Dom's chair scraped the floor as well. "I'll see you out." He waited for Sean to walk out of the kitchen and he glanced back at me. "Tell me this one thing. Did I imagine last night?"

"No."

He gave me a nod and followed Sean, leaving me snarling again. *That Sean is a self-righteous prick.*

I cleaned off the table, scraping the plates into the trash and then rinsing them for the dishwasher. Stopping in the middle of rinsing, I looked out the window above the sink. It made no sense why he would ask me to look again, *unless Dom told him he'd seen her*.

When I came upon Dom and Sean in the kitchen, Dom said he remembered a room of people. Not specifically *her*.

Arms wrapped around my middle, and I cursed myself for being so lost in thought I didn't hear them approach me. The lips that pressed against my neck were stubbly, and the five o'clock shadow scraped against my skin.

"Dom." I melted into his embrace.

His low voice purred in my ear. "What the hell happened last night, Anna?"

I couldn't stop the small giggle that came out. "What do you mean?"

His hand slid down my body and cupped my pussy. "I didn't imagine fucking this sweet pussy?"

"Mm, nope."

"Did I imagine the ritual?" he growled and nipped my ear.

"Nope." I looped my wet hands back around his neck, pulling him closer. "You loved every salacious minute." I wiggled my ass against his erection.

His arm around my waist moved, and that hand slid until he could wrap it around my throat. "What if I want to fuck you again?" He licked my neck. "What was it you told Jon?" His hand tightened around my throat. "Ah, I remember. You'd let me top."

My pussy quivered, and I felt the crotch of my shorts dampen.

"Maybe I want to eat you on the table like he did?" He bit my earlobe. "Or should I push you to your knees and face fuck you? Then again, I could bend you over and ride you like a horse that needs to be broke."

For the first time in this lifetime, I feel I've met my match. I submit to Jon or the sheriff occasionally. If the mood strikes me right. But Dom? I would love to play with him more and have him force my submission.

"Dealer's choice." I purred and pushed against his hand, teasing my wetness.

He let go of my center and directed me to the table with my throat. The minute I felt the wood against the back of my thighs, I let him push me to lie back. He released my throat and his hands looped into the waist of my shorts, ripping them from my body.

I shivered from the power I felt in the room. His demeanor told me he wouldn't take anything less than my submission at this moment. And right now? I wanted everything he planned to do to me.

His blue eyes twinkled as he pushed two fingers inside my core. "Mm, that's my girl. Wet and ready for anything."

"Am I yours now?" I tightened my pelvic floor, squeezing his fingers.

He pumped them in and out, adding a third finger. "After last night?"

"Ah, can't tell Sean the truth without going down with me." I smiled. "Play with me like you mean it."

The look in his eyes changed. That playful glimmer changed to one of pure lust, and he leaned over me, grabbing my throat again, making me moan. I felt my pussy stretch again as he added in his fourth finger.

I gasped from the stretching and let my legs fall open wider. Hell, if he grabbed a rolling pin and shoved it in one hole while he fucked me in the other, I would thank him for his ingenuity!

"So juicy." He squeezed my throat, and I felt a small gush. "You like this." He growled and leaned his head down to bite my breast through my shirt.

He pulled his fingers out, and I wheezed out a whine. "Easy girl. I'm gonna fill you back up." He used his wet hand to free his cock from his jeans. "I want to feel each of your spasms and gushes on my dick."

Dom lined up with my cunt and thrusted in hard. "Yeah!" He held himself in place and then slowly withdrew before slamming back in and bringing his moist hand to join the one already around my throat. "Now, I have it all."

His hands tightened, making me gasp for air as he thrust in and out hard. The table shook with every pump of his hips, and I loved every moment. He would release his grip and then tighten it again.

"You know, I never thought I would enjoy seeing someone I wanted fucked by someone else. But last night?" He slammed into me so hard the table moved. "Last night was everything I've ever wanted with a partner."

His hands loosened, and I wheezed out. "Even with Jon fucking your tight virgin ass?"

Dom moved his hands and gripped my nipples through my shirt. "Fuck. Yeah."

I cried out and arched my back into the pain. "Harder!"

"You tryin' to make me nut already?" He pinched them harder and pulled, making me release a long, low howl. "That's it. Show me how much you love it. I can feel your pussy get wetter with each choke, each pinch. And that makes me want to blow my load."

"Mmm, Dom." I whined, and he let go of my nipples and reached for my throat. "I want to see you fucked in every hole by a different guy."

My body trembled, and I smiled at the idea. "You pick them." I wheezed out. "I'll fuck them."

"Then I can cover you in cum. And you'll know I'm pleased with you." His voice lowered. "I could have you strapped in place and let each man take a turn. I'd want them to fill you so full, so then when I shove my cock in, it's warm and sticky." He loosened his hands.

"Like blood."

"Fuck!" He thrust in and held still, taking a deep breath. "Watching you bathe in blood and then rub me with it? Makes me sad. All I did was choke the bitches before you."

Low moans came out of me, and I felt my toes curling. "Dom!" I panted for air. "I'm so close."

"Yeah, you like how I fuck this pussy." He smiled and grabbed my throat tight as his hips bucked harder and deeper. "You can come."

My heart raced, and I couldn't get a full breath. His hands cut off my air. Panic set in as I remembered he killed the last girl this way. He grunted and sounded like a madman fucking me.

"Uhn. Uhn. Uhn. Uhn. Argh!" He slammed against me and set off my orgasm. My mouth opened to scream, but no sound came out. My body quaked and trembled and I felt my pussy twitching as I passed out.

Dominick

My body shook, and I collapsed onto Anna, panting for breath. My hands loosened from her throat and I checked for a pulse.

A breath of relief blew out hard as I found one and instead of moving, I laid there enjoying her sweet scent.

She cleared her throat about thirty seconds later and let out a moan. I felt her fingers run through my hair and I moved my head to look at her beautiful face.

"I've never met anyone like you, Anna." My voice came out soft, almost so she couldn't hear me. "Most women think I'm cold, unromantic."

"Not me. I think you're passionate." She whispered. "And now you've claimed me."

My heart raced, and I felt like I'd found someone who understood me. "I don't hear you telling me no."

"Mm. Nope." She ran her fingers down the side of my face and I pressed a kiss to her palm when it passed by my lips. "I'm not like most women."

I pushed myself up and stood over her. "That was..." I blew out another hard breath.

"Will you be coming back tonight?" She stretched and pushed herself to sit up on the table.

I shook my head and pressed my lips together. "Not tonight."

A look of anger flashed over her face. "I see."

"Anna, I need to do my job."

She slid off the table and pushed me back. "That's fine."

Anna walked away from me, leaving her pants on the floor, and went up the backstairs.

A part of me hoped she would be in my room when I got there. My hands scrubbed over my face and I heard my phone go off with a message.

Reaching into my back pocket, I pulled my phone out and rolled my eyes.

Riley: Nothing at the grocery store or Raven's. Heading to the church next.

Shit. I needed to get cleaned up and head to the police station.

After picking her pants up off the floor, I ran up the stairs to my room. There was a post-it note on the door.

Please leave the key on the dresser. Housekeeping will collect it later.

I think I broke a record for myself. Less than twenty-four hours and I've pissed a woman off so much she doesn't want to see me. *Way to go, jackass.*

Opening the door, I stomped into the room and shoved her pants along with all my clothes into my bag. Grabbed my charger from the wall and tossed the key on the dresser. I couldn't worry about her right now. I needed to focus on my job.

But my mind had other plans as I got in my car and cranked the ignition. I slammed my hands on the steering wheel in frustration and pulled out of the driveway.

The silence in the car gave me a moment to clear my head as I drove towards the Castle Hollow police station.

And that's how you ended up divorced. That little voice inside me chided.

No. Not entirely. We didn't mesh right, but when you knock your high school girlfriend up, you end up paying the consequences. Being married sucked. She sucked. Hell, I know I sucked. We were just kids and didn't have a clue what we were doing.

Stillborn. That's what they told us when she went in because she hadn't felt the baby move like it had been. After that, I focused on work and she focused on spending all my money. Then she got pregnant again. I never would've known the baby wasn't mine if her friend hadn't let it slip.

The paramedic down the road showed up to pay his respects to the new baby, and that's when Nora said it was sweet that he came to visit his kid. I had just walked in from a stakeout and after hearing that; I turned and walked out.

Shortly, she had me served with divorce papers and I gave dating a try. When I couldn't find someone compatible, I turned to hookers to take the edge off. And that's how I learned what I liked, what really got me off.

With them? I craved the fear in their eyes as I controlled their breath. The first time I went too far, I panicked and my younger brother came up with the plan. He said he knew pigs would eat anything. So that's what we did.

I tried to be careful after that, and I had done well until about six months ago. That skinny little bitch whined like a newborn puppy. I lost my temper. I called up Anthony, and he fed his pigs again.

"Well, this has been a great trip down memory lane." I snarled, blew out a hard breath, as I parked at the Castle Hollow police department and got out of my car.

Concrete surrounded the station, and there were signs pointing where to go for the jail or for the sheriff. I walked over to the door for the sheriff and went inside, where an older woman sat at a desk.

"Welcome to the Castle Hollow police department. Can I help you?"

"I'm Detective Dominick Moody from Grimgate. I need to see if Sheriff Lincoln is available."

She smiled and motioned for me to take a seat while she lifted the receiver off her phone and called him. She spoke so quietly I didn't hear a word she said, but she waved me back over. "You wanna go down this hall." She pointed to her right. "And he's the last door on the left."

"Thank you." I leaned back and spied the nameplate on her desk. "Miss Josie."

"Shucks, a handsome man like you shouldn't be flirting with the likes of me. But I'll take it."

I chuckled as I went around her desk to the hall and followed it down to the sheriff. With two quick knocks on his open door and he waved me in.

"Close that so we can talk." He gave me a nod.

I closed the door behind me and took a seat. He leaned back in his chair and eyed me before he spoke. "What brings you here?"

"Well, sheriff, Detective Sean Riley and myself have been tasked with some missing girls and a cold case that happened thirty years ago here in Castle Hollow."

"The Bishop case." He nodded. "What can I do for you?"

"Let's start with the missing girls." I pulled the pictures from my jacket and handed them to him. "Do you recognize any of them?"

While he reviewed them, I looked around his office. There were department photos in frames, a couple little league pennants, and a few framed articles from local papers. His wooden desk looked old and worn, complete with some graffiti carved into it.

He made a little humming sound with each picture he reviewed. "Nope. Can't say as I do."

"Are you sure?" I sat forward in my chair.

He narrowed his eyes and looked at me. "Do you want me to look again?"

I held my hands up in defense. "I'm just trying to be sure."

"Mm-hmm." He glowered my way and looked at the pictures again. "No. No. No. And no." He handed them back to me. "Anything else?"

I had to remind myself to take a deep breath, and that this man had seen me naked.

"Do you remember the Bishop case? Was there anything strange about the case?" I sat back and relaxed in the chair. It wasn't as comfy as my memory foam back in Grimgate, but it felt decent enough. "Anything that stands out?"

He shook his head. "I remember sweet Anna having to hear that her parents were dead on her birthday and Miss Ramona was distraught over losing her daughter. There was no weapon, no prints, nothing."

My head cocked to the side. "What could get in and do that?"

"Well. Maybe a specter." He laughed.

"Or a demon?" I waited to see his reaction.

He laughed harder. "Now you're really not going to accuse Jon of something like that? Are you?"

"I don't know the guy..." The sheriff cut me off.

"But you let him suck your dick and fuck your ass." He winked. "Now, does he strike you as the killing kind?"

My jaw hit the ground. "I... uh... no." I cleared my throat. "No."

"That's right. He's a lover." He put his hands behind his head. "Now. Since you're talking about cases, I got one for you." Taking his hands down, he sat forward and picked up a file that had been sitting in front of him and tossed it across the desk. "One of our residents, Miss Joann Helms, is missing her niece. She was a sweet young thing named Brooke, and she was last seen in Ailmere at a no-tell motel there with a man."

I picked up the file and flipped it open. In an instant, I recognized the young woman in the picture, but Brooke wasn't the name she gave me. She told me her name was Candy. And my life came to a screeching halt at that moment.

He knows. And this is his way of putting me on notice.

"I've talked to all the people I could and looked into her disappearance. All I have left to do is go out to the motel and see if there's surveillance."

"I could do that for you." I offered, and closed the file. "Help you out."

He scratched his chin. "You sure? I don't want to put you out."

"It's not a problem. I'm heading back to Grimgate this afternoon."

He nodded and smiled at me. "Good deal."

I stood up from my chair and smiled. "I'll be in touch."

"See that you do." The smile that crossed his face made him look evil.

Taking my leave from his office, I waved at the sweet secretary and went back to my car. I sat in the driver's seat for a few minutes before I texted Sean.

Me: Finished with the sheriff. Nothing new. What's left?

Riley: The Salty Chef. Meet there?

Me: On my way.

I tossed my phone in the passenger seat, put on my seatbelt and drove through town, passing the Serene Raven on the way to the diner. Before I got out of the car, I grabbed my phone and found the number for the inn.

After pushing the call button on the phone number from the website, I waited to hear her voice.

"Serene Raven." A deep male voice answered.

"May I speak to Anna, please?"

"Of course. Who may I say is calling?"

"Dom."

"Oh, hello detective!" Jon's voice filled my ear and I couldn't help smiling at how happy he sounded to hear my voice. "Give me just a moment."

He wasn't mad at me for leaving. Why was she?

"This is Anna."

Hearing her voice made my cock painfully hard in my jeans. "Anna." My voice whispered into the phone. "Why are you mad?"

"I'm not."

"When I left, I thought you were mad."

"Oh. That? Sorry detective, I wanted more and since you had to leave, I went to my room to play with myself."

"Oh." My eyes blinked a few times and my cock throbbed harder in my pants.

"Do you want details?" Her voice dropped to a low and sultry tone. "I fingered my clit and used my glass dildo to fill my wet pussy up, but it didn't feel as good as you."

"Anna. If I jack off in the car in the parking lot of the Salty Chef, I'll be arrested for indecent exposure."

Her laughter warmed my body like a good whiskey. "Then I guess you'll have to call me later."

"You got it, babe." I rubbed the outside of my jeans and willed my cock to go down.

"Till tonight, Dom." She blew a kiss on the phone and the call disconnected.

This woman might be the end of me.

Dominick

When I walked into the diner, the small bell on the door jingled and everyone inside looked my way. The smell of burgers and bbq punched me in the gut and my mouth watered from the smells.

The restaurant itself reminded me of an old fifties style diner with its bright red booths and chairs and black and white checked floor and service counter with stools. They decorated the walls with cute sayings and memorabilia.

After five years of being partnered with Sean, I knew where to look for him. He always liked to sit in the back of restaurants so he could watch the entire place in case something happened, and he liked to be close to the bathrooms.

Sean waved me over, and I went to join him at a table near the back. As I slid into the booth, a young woman in a short black skirt and white blouse appeared and set a glass of water down for me.

Her legs were long, and she had on puffy socks, the kind most women prefer on cold days, and her blouse was unbuttoned at the top. "Welcome to The Salty Chef. I'm Maddie and I'll be your server today."

"Thank you, Maddie." Sean smiled at her and leaned closer to her. "We'll need a few minutes."

"Sure thing." She did this little curtsy and wandered off.

I noticed Sean's eyes following her, and I laughed. "Easy old man. You're probably old enough to be her granddad."

He turned to me with a grimace on his face. "And?"

And? That was his response?

I turned to look behind me where Maddie refilled coffee for another couple and then back at Sean.

"Like 'em young?"

"I like them legal." He snapped defensively and picked up his menu.

I did the same, but my mind churned over one question. *How well does anyone know anybody?* Last night Anna, Jon, the sheriff and the other guy let me in to have a good time with them, but they didn't know me. They didn't know *who* I was on my own time.

It occurred to me then that wasn't the first time they partied like that. They all were very comfortable with each other and, for God knows what reason, I felt like I belonged there as well.

"They have ribs." Sean patted his small belly. "I think that's what I want."

Maddie strolled over to us. "Are you gentlemen ready?"

"I think we are, doll." He gave her a wink. "I'll have the half rack of ribs, with extra sauce on the side."

She jotted it down on her little notepad and looked at me. "And for you, Detective Moody?"

I looked up at her curiously. "Have we met?"

She giggled and her cheeks pinked up. "No. You met my grandpa last night at Miss Anna's."

"Gotcha." I smiled back. "I'll have a burger and fries."

"What would you like on it?" She glanced at Sean and her cheeks reddened further.

"Run it through the garden, kiddo."

She let out another giggle and covered her mouth with the order pad. "I'm older than you think."

"I'm sure you are." I nodded and handed her both menus. "Thank you."

She walked away slowly, swinging her hips, and Sean reached up to adjust his tie. I sat back and put my arm on the back of the booth and waited for him to get his head back in the game.

When he finally sat back, he looked over at me with a silly grin on his face. "So, I got nothing from anyone everywhere I went. How'd it go with Sheriff Lincoln?"

You dirty old man.

"Good. He said nothing stood out about the Bishop case and that he hadn't seen the girls. Then he tossed another case at me for a missing girl."

Sean chuffed out a breath. "Another one?"

"Yeah, some girl from here went missing in Ailmere at the no-tell-motel."

Sean laughed. "Nobody goes to one of those unless they're up to no good."

I remembered parking my car at a restaurant and walking over to meet her. She happened to be at the same bar I frequented when I didn't want to sit at home alone. We talked, she got handsy, I asked if she wanted to go somewhere private, she tossed a number at me and we kissed to seal the deal.

I didn't want to be seen where I live going into the motel there, so I suggested the one in Ailmere. Being a bigger city than Grimgate, we wouldn't be noticed. We left the bar; she gave me a handjob behind the building and then told me to hurry because the clock was ticking.

All I wanted that night was to get my dick wet, get my rocks off, and go home. The sex sucked. I squeezed too hard for too long and, well, that was that.

Reaching up, I scratched my scruff. "Yeah. Well. I told him I'd go check out the surveillance cameras for him."

"Look at you." He lifted his water in a toast. "Making friends."

"Fuck off, man." I half laughed. "Isn't that part of the job? Work together with the local PD's?"

"Yeah. But no one does." He stared at me for a moment, then leaned in over the table. "I still don't understand why you think you saw one of the missing girls."

I sat up and met him halfway. "Because I kept staring at the damn pictures."

He raised an eyebrow and sat back. *Damn my mouth!* I'm not sure how I'm going to get him to stop asking, but that's something for later. As Maddie walked up with our food, she gave us another smile and served us and wandered off.

The ribs were so tender the meat fell off the bone and when he took his first bite; he moaned. "Damn, that's good!"

I laughed at him, salted my burger and arranged it so I could pick it up and take a bite. After laughing at him, I felt like an asshole when I moaned as well. "This is a damn juicy burger!"

Neither of us spoke as we gobbled up our food like some cave dwellers. Maddie came around and brought more napkins and fresh water, but we were too focused on eating to care or use manners.

When we finished, Sean excused himself to the bathroom to clean off the barbeque sauce, and I sat back with my water. Looking to my left, the old man from last night walked around, talking to the few other patrons. When our eyes met, he smiled and came over to me.

"Dom!" He shook my hand. "Good to see you again."

What was it the sheriff called him? Oleg? Ollie? Ollin!

"Hey Ollin. How's business?" I took my hand back and turned in my seat to see him better.

"Not bad. Not bad." He winked at me. "I didn't know you were one of us."

"I'm sorry." I tilted my head. "What do you mean?"

A flashback slapped me upside the head as I remembered the sheriff saying, "I think he's almost done playing with his food."

I pointed to my plate. "From last night?"

A big smile swept across the old man's face as he nodded and I had to fight the urge to vomit. I pointed over my shoulder to where the police station was. "He knows?" My words came out in a whisper.

Ollin took a seat across from me at the table. "You don't know much about Castle Hollow, do you?"

"Well, I've heard the rumors and myths."

He nodded his head towards the couple in the opposite corner from us. "They're rougarou. Like their parents before them and their grandparents before that. They need it to survive, sure they eat other things, but long pig is best." He motioned to the person sitting at the counter. "Pete there just likes the taste and enjoys popping in for a special now and then."

And everybody's okay with this?

I scratched my forehead and looked at him with my eyes narrowed. "Does Anna? What is Anna?"

"Oh, no, she just uses the blood, saves me a step. And she's not a what. She's a who." He smiled. "Do you believe in reincarnation?"

I glanced around Ollin toward the back where the bathrooms were, looking for Sean. "That's something the hippie dippy folks think."

"Is it?" He laughed, noticing me looking around. "Looking for your buddy?"

"He's my partner."

"He's a pedo." Ollin's face lost all joy. "Maddie used a glamor spell. She said he looked like the man who hit on one of her friends."

Ignoring the spell part, I focused on what I felt was more important as I felt the blood drain from my face. "He what?"

Ollin leaned in and folded his hands on the table. "Listen, Dom, I like you. I'm not sure what it is, but I think you might be one of us. The dark ones. We let the light in, but we live in the darkness."

I copied his gesture and leaned in. "Is everyone in this town a... a... deviant?"

He shrugged and his lips frowned. "What is a deviant?" He tilted his head. "Society says we have to do and act the way they want to be accepted." He pointed his finger down on the table, stressing his next words. "But here? In Castle Hollow? We take care of our own in *our* society." Ollin lifted a finger in acknowledgement of the rougarou couple and scooted out of the booth. "Good chat."

"Yeah." I nodded. "Thanks."

Ollin walked over to them and Maddie came through the kitchen doors to the front counter and then Sean came walking down the hall, whistling.

"What took you so long?" I looked up at him and felt my skin crawl, being in his presence.

"I hit the head, man. Sometimes things take time." He reached for his water. "You ready to go?"

I nodded and threw some bills on the table as a tip, then went up to pay. This time I watched Sean's actions. He gave Maddie a lecherous smile and stroked her hand when he gave her the money. "Thank you." He took his change from her. "For everything."

Her face paled, and she nodded with a wane smile. "You're welcome."

He walked over to the door, and I held out a twenty for her. "Oh, no need. Grandpa said yours was on the house."

"Tell Ollin thank you." After a quick nod, I put my money away and then looked at her again. "Sweetheart? How old are you?"

"I'm nineteen." She whispered and looked over at Sean's back with disgust.

I scratched my head and nodded at her. What could I say to make things better? Right now? Nothing. I needed to do some digging. Sure, I may have accidentally choked a few girls to death. But they were legal. If Sean's playing with underage ones, I need proof.

Anna

Jon finished cleaning up the yard, and I took my time cleaning the room I put Dom in. In between cleaning, we had three couples check-in. They called themselves "ghost hunters". The thought of them traipsing around in the woods had me cackling while I vacuumed.

If they could find the supernatural, it would be here in Castle Hollow. But being around Jon didn't set their little machines off. What happened to people just trusting instinct or, hell, believing what they wanted?

Everyone wants proof of everything these days, well that's not true. The people who come here for tarot readings trust what I tell them. Some come back for more. Others want potions to help. But my favorite are the ones who wanted to learn.

Once I finished with the vacuum, I put it away and grabbed the fresh linens for the room, along with new toiletries and towels. I stuck with the family's theme of plain white for them all because sometimes bleach needed to be used and no one likes dull colors.

I behaved badly earlier with Dom. I shouldn't have walked away. It's not like me to behave that way either. And I'm not sure which craved his attention more. My heart or my pussy. But here I was pining over a man I just met.

"Anna?" Jon's voice pulled me from my thoughts.

"Yes, darling?" I spun to face him and opened my arms for a hug.

He walked into my arms and wrapped himself around me. "He'll be back."

"How can you be so sure?" I looked up into his eyes.

Jon smiled and caressed the side of my face with his fingers. "Because he can be himself with us."

"True." I broke free of our hold and took his hand to lead him out of the room.

We ambled down the hall, and I glanced at the old paintings. Victorian women in varied positions, looking prim and proper, and I thought back to my youth. I always wanted to be one of those women.

At the end of the hall, just outside our room, hung a painting of me as Countess Bathory. I remember sitting for the painting. The uncomfortable straight-backed position of sitting on a hard chair for hours!

In the portrait I had on the same gown I saw in my regression. Deep burgundy with gold embroidery. Tight corset lifting my bosom high. Bright cheeks, sharp nose, full red lips. I looked so regal and proper.

Shortly after this commissioned painting, people accused me of the killings and they confined me to my house in arrest.

"You were beautiful then." Jon raised our hands and pointed to the painting. "But now? You're drop dead gorgeous." He brought our hands to his mouth and pressed a kiss to the back of my hand.

"Thank you." I opened the door and pulled him inside.

He kicked the door closed and whipped me around, capturing my lips with his, holding me close. As we pulled back, I pushed my bottom lip out in a mock pout.

With a sigh, I looked up at him. "I did something petty."

He raised an eyebrow at me. "What did you do?"

"I may have called Hugh and told him what I saw in my vision of Dom."

Jon's eyes opened wide. "You threw him to Hugh?"

My eyes closed as I nodded my head. "I told you it was petty."

"It was." He stepped back. "Do you want me to talk to Hugh?"

"No. What will be, will be." I shook my head and looked over at the nightstand where our alarm clock sat. "I have a reading to get to."

He gave me a nod and then smiled wickedly. "I'm going to fuck with the ghost hunters."

That had my head falling back with a belly laugh. "I love you."

"I love you too, my sweet Countess." He bowed and left the room, closing the door behind him softly.

Maddie wouldn't be here for her reading until her shift ended at The Salty Chef, which gave me time to shower and let the negativity wash down the drain.

I smelled like a heady mix of sex and sweat. No one needed to smell that except for my inner circle of lovers. Stripping off my clothes, I tossed them into the hamper that sat by the door and I peered at myself in the mirror.

High, perky breasts that didn't need a bra with small dusty rose nipples topping them. Not one stretch mark to be seen. My flawless porcelain skin naturally indented at the waist, giving me an hour-glass figure and my hips spread wide enough that when I walked with a sway, everyone took notice.

My favorite reincarnation had me with thick curves and breasts so full they hung like udders when I was on my knees. Jon introduced me to the fun one could have with such big mommy milkers and, boy, did we have fun.

I didn't like being pregnant or raising the little brat. A chuckle filled the room as I turned to the side to admire myself more. They stretched my body in ways I couldn't control and having to tend to the child cut into my playtime.

Maybe that was selfish of me, but at least I knew my own limits. Some never give thought to their limits and then are stuck with the consequences of their actions.

I turned again and looked over my shoulder to admire my backside. Smooth skin and a heart-shaped ass that drove men wild. My teeth bit into my bottom lip as I made the muscles dance and twerk.

Other people use plastic surgeons, me? I prefer my beauty routine to be organic. I gave myself a cheeky wink and walked to the bathroom when the main phone rang. After two rings, I knew Jon answered it and I got out my towels.

I heard the bedroom door open, and Jon poked his head in. "Our handsome detective is calling for you."

"Ugh. Tell him I'll call him back." I stuck my head out of the bathroom and looked at him.

He shook his head. "Take the call."

"Fine." I laughed and leaned against the door frame. "I just wanted to take a shower."

He tilted his head and flicked his forked tongue out, lapping at the air. "You smell fuckable."

"Later." I winked and walked out of the bathroom and around the bed to sit down. I tossed my hair behind my shoulders and lifted the receiver. "This is Anna."

"Anna." His voice whispered into the phone. "Why are you mad?"

His soft voice melted something inside of me and my voice softened to meet his. "I'm not."

"When I left, I thought you were mad."

"Oh. That?" I tried to play dumb, but then I gave him the truth mixed with a tease. "Sorry detective, I wanted more and since you had to leave, I went to my room to play with myself."

"Oh." His husky voice filled my ear, and I swung my body around onto the bed, spreading my legs.

I dropped my voice to a low, sultry tone. "Do you want details?" My free hand slid down my body and teased my clit. "I fingered my clit and used my glass dildo to fill my wet pussy up, but it didn't feel as good as you."

"Anna. If I jack off in the car in the parking lot of the Salty Chef, I'll be arrested for indecent exposure." His voice sounded desperate, and that made my pussy quiver.

I laughed softly and reveled in the knowledge I had such an effect on him. "Then I guess you'll have to call me later."

"You got it, babe."

"Till tonight, Dom." I blew a kiss into the phone and set the receiver back on its cradle.

I like when Jon's right about something.

Now it's time to shower and get ready to meet Maddie.

Dominick

After leaving the diner, I drove over to the Castle Hollow Heritage Library and grabbed my briefcase from the backseat.

My laptop and old case notes were inside and I needed a place where I could go back over them in private and still have access to some archives.

I knew I could've gone back to the station or home to work, but I needed to do this where Sean wouldn't be able to randomly pop over or see what I was doing.

Walking up the sidewalk, I passed a young woman with her toddler in tow and smiled politely at them before entering the large brick building.

Books give off the most appealing smell and I inhaled the scent deeply as I walked over to the main desk and smiled at the white-haired, short lady who reminded me of my grandma.

"Why hello there, welcome to the Heritage Library. What can I do for you?" She pushed her glasses up her nose and smiled back at me.

"Do you have an open study room I could use?"

"Sure thing." She pointed toward the back of the library. "Take your pick of any that are open."

"Wonderful." I leaned my head to the side to see her name tag. "Thank you, Olga."

She gave me a quick nod and went back to checking in books.

I walked through the open lobby area, admiring the layout and the atmosphere. Off to the right, the children's section caught my eye. Bright colors, Lego tables, stuffed animals and plenty of seating for small people.

They had a setup before the stacks for computer use. Ten terminals in total and four had people using them.

Then I chose an aisle and walked between the large shelves of books, glancing at some titles and remembering when I had to spend long hours in a library studying. Sometimes I missed those days, simpler days.

At the end of the aisle, the back wall had five doors all propped open. These were the small study rooms and to my left, I noticed a larger room with the door closed.

A glass wall made up the front of the room so you could see the people inside.

I took the room farthest from the group in case they got loud. My investigation into Sean needed my full focus, and I closed the door behind me to ensure no distractions.

Opening my briefcase, I pulled out my computer and plugged it in, then pulled out my files and a notebook. I sat in the hard wooden chair and my fingers flew over the keys, typing in my password.

While the computer went through its opening processes, I jotted down how long he disappeared for at the restaurant and Maddie's demeanor before and after that time. I also noted what Ollin told me. That she believed he was the man who hit on her friend.

Next I went to excel and pulled my up my case spreadsheet and clicked to organize them by case nature. It neatly grouped together all the cases with young girls for me. My next command grouped them chronologically.

I blew out a breath and opened the file on our most recent case, Ella Collins, and I reread the notes inside. We were always together when we talked to her, so she wouldn't be what I need. I need to find girls he spoke to alone.

Closing that file, I went to the next one. LaTasha Haynes. I remembered her well. In my notes, I found her to be a delightful girl to talk to. She had chubby cheeks, witty humor and answered our questions even when she cried from the memories.

In between my notes, I highlighted when Sean and I spoke to her and her parents individually.

"BINGO!"

I set the file aside and moved on to the next case, Hollie Callahan, and found the same highlight, making me growl and toss that file with LaTasha's.

Now that I knew what I needed to look for, I went through the small stack of case notes faster and found three more girls. Nina Russell, Pamela Glover and Deanna Maynard. With each case I reviewed, anger grew inside me.

As I sat back in the chair, I rubbed my eyes and then my fist came down on the desk in anger. Hearsay is one thing. Looking deeper into what you hear is what helps you decide what to do. For me, in this moment, finding five young girls that he "may have" said or done something untoward with made me sick.

I needed to talk to these five girls. I needed to find out if he was a pedophile. And if he was? Well, I'll make sure he never preys on a young girl again.

The door opened at the same time I asked the room. "Why did I overlook this?"

"Overlook what?" Jon came in and sat across from me at the table. "You don't have to talk if you don't want to. I just popped into the library to hang up a flyer and I noticed your car outside."

"How well do you know me?" I tilted my head and watched him brush his hand through his blond hair.

"That's an existential question." He laughed. "How well does anyone know anybody?"

I gave a half-hearted chuckle. "You're not wrong."

"Pardon me for saying, but you look very distressed." He tilted his head, and I watched his eyes soften. "Can I help with anything?"

"What would you do if you met someone who was a pedophile?"

Jon's head fell back in laughter. "I'd torture them and make sure they died a bloody death." He nodded. "When Anna was thirteen, she felt our connection, and I told her I wouldn't cross that line."

"A demon with morals, huh?"

"Dom, I am many things. But I do not prey on children."

"Good to know." The tension in my shoulders eased as I talked with him. "How old are you?"

His laughter grew. "I'm immortal. Time means nothing to me."

"How long have you known Anna?" I collected my files and put them back in my briefcase.

"I first met her in the fifteen hundreds when she was known as Countess Bathory."

My hand froze in place and I looked at his face to see if this might be his idea of a joke. When I saw how serious he looked, I sat back and stared at him.

"Perhaps you should do a regression to see who you were."

"You're the second person today to mention reincarnation to me." I shut my computer down. "I didn't believe in it, but considering I know a demon."

"Intimately." He winked at me.

"I get the feeling you're goading me into believing I've lived before?" I closed the laptop and unplugged it, putting it on top of the files.

Jon sat with a smile on his face. "You have. Twice."

"Are you saying you know me?" I laughed, still finding the idea of reincarnation absurd.

He stood up and tucked a hand into the pocket of his jeans. "The first time you almost gave into your predilection, the second you fought it." He turned and opened the door. "This time, you're embracing it."

I felt the blood drain from my face. *How could he know about my dark side? I mean the sex part he knows, but all of it?*

"We'll put a plate of dinner aside for you for when you get home." He walked out and closed the door behind him.

I watched him leave, then finished putting my things away and propped the door open for the next person.

I had a young girl to speak with and no time to waste.

Anna

My tarot reading with Maddie left me feeling dirty.

Jon wasn't home. He went to distribute flyers for the next past-life regression class he does. The crazy ghost hunters were asleep because they claim ghosts are easier to film and find at night.

Left alone to my own devices, I pulled my *Book of Shadows* out and scrutinized every spell looking for one that would be perfect for Detective Sean Riley, but I had yet to find one that had the right pain level.

When I first sat down with Maddie, she told me about meeting Dom and what a gentleman he had been. Then she clammed up and said she needed to know what the cards had to say.

I owned several decks, but I had one deck that remained my favorite. They were well used, so the colors weren't bold and bright on them anymore. But the artwork always held my interest. When looking at them each on their own, I could still find new things that amazed me.

The deck created by Aleister Crowley could be brutal, and over the years of study with them I've learned that each card works together to paint the reading for me. Just because I see a death card doesn't mean a death. It could symbolize a new beginning or the end of something.

Something this deck excelled at? The truth. I mean, they will tell you how it is without a sugar coating. Some people liked that. That's what they needed from the reading, but most touristy people only wanted fluff and good things.

I shuffled the cards to clear them and then handed the deck to Maddie to shuffle, and I watched her as she focused. For a young woman, her aura appeared muddled and broken. She finished shuffling and handed them back to me.

The moment I flipped the first two cards, I saw the broken heart and betrayal of someone in power. Flipping the next four, I saw her trying to do something good and having it backfire, which filled her with fear. I laid the last four out and saw a "knight in shining armor" coming to her rescue.

Tapping my fingers against the table, I looked her in the eyes and asked the obvious question I had. "Who hurt you?"

A single tear fell down her cheek, and she shook her head.

"Well, here's what I see. You feel betrayed by someone in power because you were trying to do something to help someone you care about. That backfired, causing you to be hurt and you're afraid." I reached for her hand and held it in mine. "Sweetheart, you need to tell someone who hurt you. If you keep it silent, nothing can be done."

"I know." She wiped the side of her face on her shoulder. "Do you remember Trina?"

A young girl with long blond hair, rosy cheeks and bright blue eyes popped into my head. "I do. She works at your grandpa's diner." I snapped my fingers. "Hey, didn't she win Miss Pumpkin at last year's fall festival?"

"She did." She took a deep breath. "Well, she went to the movies over in Kilton. It was an afternoon matinee. She loves old movies." Maddie smiled at me for a moment, then frowned. "She said an old man came in and they talked before the movie."

"I'm following along so far." I gave her hand a squeeze.

She took a deep breath in and let it out slowly before continuing. "Well, he stepped out about twenty minutes into the movie and when he came back, he changed where he was sitting so he could sit next to her."

"And they were the only two in the theater?"

She nodded. "It was fine for part of the movie. Then he put his arm around her, and you know how the arm rests move? He put it up and touched her. She said he covered her mouth with his hand."

"You mean from the one he had around her?" I felt my face scrunch up uncomfortably.

"Yeah. The other hand touched her all over." Tears flowed from her eyes.

I knew she was in pain sharing this with me, and I hated seeing her hurt.

"So he made her do stuff to him and when the movie was over, he threatened her not to tell or he'd come for her." Maddie looked around and I reached over for a box of tissues, putting them on the table. "Then she saw him after school one day and he made this motion of watching her and drove off."

"What a dick." My jaw clenched in anger. "I'm not mad at you."

"Oh, I know, Miss Anna." She took her hand from mine so she could blow her nose. "So then when I saw that, I asked what happened, and she finally told me."

"When did this happen?"

"Last year. And today she saw the car in town and she was sure it was him who came into the diner with Dom. I had her stay in back away from everyone with Uncle Dean. Then I used a glamor, and I did it just like you taught me to make myself look younger..." Her voice trailed off.

Bile rose in my throat and my voice came out gravelly. "Did he touch you? I don't need details. I just need to know."

Her head bobbed, and she broke down in body shaking sobs. I jumped from my chair and kneeled at her feet, pulling her into my arms.

The motherfucker is going to die.

I rocked her gently, and that's where Jon found us when he returned. He said nothing as he joined up and wrapped us both in his arms, rocking with us.

Dominick

The city sign for Kilton welcomed me and during my drive, I thought of the many ways to inflict pain on a person.

Needles through tender areas, like his dick. A branding iron on his face. Disembowelment. Ripping off finger and toenails. Tearing his asshole wide open.

They were all good. And I hadn't come up with one that I felt could be dismissed.

My anger flared every time I looked back at situations and wrote off his behavior. More than once I'd noticed him looking at women. I just never paid attention to the ages. Everyone looked at someone who looked good.

The bile in my throat rose, and I knew I couldn't fight Chuck running the elevator up anymore. I pulled over to the side of the road and fumbled opening my car door, scrambling from the driver's seat around my car to wretch on the side of the road. With each heave, I felt angrier.

What the fuck was wrong with him?

"Unh!" My abdomen tightened, pushing more up. "Ugh!" Again. "Ass!" I dropped to my knees in the gravel.

"Hole!" My right hand slammed against the ground to hold my body up from face-planting in my vomit.

Five fucking years and I missed it.

I took two deep breaths and sat back on my heels, wiping my forehead with the back of my arm.

My head fell back, and I watched the clouds drift by before I tried standing up. My body shook from the violence of expelling everything I'd ever eaten in my whole forty-four years. I popped open my trunk and took out a bottle of water to rinse and spit, then I sipped some down.

I leaned back on my car and took in the scenery. Driving into Kilton, the back-way wasn't as bad as guys at the station made it sound. Sure, the dense forest of trees looked spooky, kind of like they were moving. But overall, the scene took my breath away.

Once my body felt like it stopped quivering, I got back in my car, chucked the water bottle in the backseat to join the plastic bottle graveyard I had going in my car and followed my GPS to Hollie Callahan's house.

The case we worked with the Callahan's seemed to be a basic b and e. The burglars came in through her window and one held a knife to her throat while the other did a smash and grab while her parents weren't home.

In each of the cases with young girls, if we divided and conquered, he took the child. His reasoning was since he had kids, he knew how to talk to them.

My stomach rolled again, and I half laughed. "Oh, no. There's nothing left."

The small city of Kilton couldn't be bigger than ten blocks by ten blocks. As soon as I turned onto the street where their house sat, I recognized where I was. I pulled up in front of the blue and white ranch-style house complete with the manicured lawn, killed my engine and then dug a mint out of my center console to help my breath.

My hand ran through my dark hair and I took one last deep breath before exiting the vehicle. The walk up to the door felt like a prison sentence. Investigating my partner wasn't supposed to be something I had to do.

Trust. We should be able to trust each other. But something deep in my gut told me what I would find.

I lifted my hand to knock, and the door flew open. "Detective Moody." Eliza Callahan looked at me. "What brings you here?"

"I thought I would check in and see how your family's doing and see how Hollie..." I stopped speaking because of the tears pouring from her eyes. "Missus Callahan?"

She waved her hands around like some women do to stop crying. "Ha..." She shook her head, and I saw her husband come up and he placed his hands on her shoulders.

"I got this, Liz."

She patted his hands and jogged away while he stepped outside with me and closed the door.

He patted his chest a couple times and instead of the firm voice I remembered; a choked one took its place. "Hollie..." His chest shuddered. "She killed herself three months ago."

"Mister Callahan, there are no words..." I swallowed hard. "I'm so sorry for your loss."

"Thank you."

"I didn't know." I took a step back.

"No. There's no way you could've." He held out his hand, and I accepted the shaking with him.

What do you say to people who've just lost their child? I had no clue, and being at such a loss, so I backed away and headed back to my car.

He lifted his hand in a wave and I stuck my key in the ignition and turned. My engine roared to life, and I pulled away from the curb.

The Russell's also had a case with a young girl a couple of blocks over. Same burglary and between both houses, we caught the boys who were doing it.

This place stood out to me for how perfect all the lawns were. I remembered being called in on the case because they had stumped the police chief. There were no cameras on residential houses, only the parks had some.

I turned the corner and drove to the and of the block. There were two girls outside playing basketball. When they noticed my car, they walked up into the yard.

Pulling over to the curb, I parked in front of the house with the kids, killed the engine and got out.

"Hey! Detective Moody!" A girl jogged over, and I recognized Nina right away.

"Hey yourself, Nina." I smiled. "Are your parents' home?"

"Nope." She rolled her eyes. "It's date night."

I laughed, and she dribbled the basketball. “Whatcha need?”

“Well, I had a question for you, but I need to wait for your parents.”

She shrugged her shoulders and took a shot at the hoop. “You can ask me.” She caught the rebound and went for a lay-up. “You remember Naomi, my older sister. She’s legal.”

The older sister walked over. “She’s right. I’m here.”

I nodded and looked down at the ground. “I should come back.”

“Tell him.” I heard Naomi whisper harshly.

“Tell me what?” I walked closed and partially sat on my hood.

Nina’s eyes shifted around, and she puffed her cheeks out with the breath she blew out. “Can you keep this between us?”

“As long as you’re not in danger.” I nodded. “I can do that.”

“Okay, look. The other dude?”

“My partner? Riley?” I tilted my head and watched her nervously sway.

She nodded. “He’s creepy. Like. Really creepy.”

I folded my bottom lip into my mouth and let my tongue wet it. “Did he do something to you?”

The sisters shared a look, then Naomi stepped closer and held Nina’s hand. “It’s okay.”

That motherfucker. I felt my nostrils flare.

"If it'll be easier, you can nod. I won't ask questions." I kept my voice soft and hoped none of my anger came through.

She nodded and looked up at me in tears. "He... hurt my friend, too."

Well, shit.

I took a stab in the dark. "Hollie?"

She nodded, and her sister hugged her.

"I promise. I won't let him hurt anyone else." I shuddered out a breath. "You have my word."

Naomi gave me a half smile. "Thank you."

I pushed off the hood of my car and playing with my keys in my hand. "Do your parents know?"

"Yeah. But Nina refused to file a report."

I pulled my wallet from my back pocket and flipped it open, pulling out a business card, and handed it to Naomi. "Call me if something happens."

She let out a sigh of relief. "Thanks for being one of the good guys."

"You bet. And Nina?" I peered around her sister to look her in the eyes. "You have my word."

Nina let go of Naomi and wrapped her arms around me. "Thank you."

When she released me, I got back in my car and watched the girls go inside the house. Then I turned my car around and headed back to Castle Hollow.

Anna

The mighty ghost hunters were off in the woods hunting for the supernatural, which gave me time to rage inside the inn.

"I know who I am. I know what I am. But I would never hurt a child!" I spun and threw a dirty plate at the wall. It shattered upon impact, sending shards all over the kitchen.

Jon sat quietly at the table, seething.

"Say something!" I slammed my hands on the table.

He lifted his shoulders casually. "He must die."

"And not quickly." I pushed off and paced the floor like a caged animal. "That would be too good for him."

The main door opened, setting off the small chime to alert us, and Dom's voice echoed in the foyer. "Anna! Jon!"

"Kitchen!" Jon called back and sat forward with his hands folded on the table, watching for Dom to enter.

His footfalls were heavy and quick and when he entered the kitchen, I saw the anger on his face. Before I could say a word, Jon spoke.

"Your suspicions were confirmed."

"I am so pissed right now." He snarled and reached up to pull his hair. "And disgusted."

"As am I." I stepped closer. "What has you bothered?"

"You are both hunting the same animal." Jon's voice whispered, and my eyes widened.

"Your piece of shit partner hurt other girls?" I growled and grabbed a cup, sending it flying at the back door.

"Who?" He demanded and stepped up to me, grabbing my shoulders. "Who else did he touch, Anna?"

A sardonic laugh came out as I gritted my teeth. "Two of ours. And for that, he will die."

His hands loosened. "No." His head shook. "Tell me not Maddie."

My eyes narrowed. "How did you know?" I brought my arms up and knocked his hands from my body before shoving him back. "How the fuck did you know?"

Dom blew out a hard breath. "It was his behavior that made me wonder. Then he disappeared at the diner for a significant amount of time and when Maddie returned, she was different. Almost broken."

"Tis true, Countess." Jon sat back. "I found Dom at the library researching."

"I left the library and went to talk to one girl, but she..." He dropped to his knees. "She committed suicide." Tears streaked down his cheeks. "So I checked on another girl and she gave me the confirmation I needed." Dom lifted his head and his yell shook the frames on the wall.

"Your services won't be needed." I scowled. "We take care of our own."

In the blink of an eye, he jumped up from the floor and wrapped his hand around my throat, holding me tight. "I. Am. Your. Kind."

Darkness flashed in his blue eyes, and his face changed before my eyes. His hairline moved, giving him a deep widow's peak, and it had replaced his wavy locks with shorter, lighter hair. His nose grew to a long point and his lips flattened.

I gasped for air and grabbed his arm. My voice tried to come out, but his hold was too strong. I knew why I felt connected to him. It wasn't only the darkness inside us, and before blackness filled my vision, I saw a blast from my past.

Dominick

Anna went limp under my hold. I released her throat and caught her, holding her tight against me.

"Dammit! My anger got the best of me." I whispered and felt Jon at my back.

His finger traced down my spine, giving me the chills before his hand cupped my shoulder. "Come. Let's lay her down."

It took some adjusting to scoop her up in my arms, and then I turned and followed Jon up the steps and down the hall. He opened the large oak door at the end of the hall and step aside to allow me to pass by him.

After he closed the door, he flipped on the lights, and awe filled me. The large king bed served as a focal piece and a place to sleep. The comforter on top of the bed reminded me of a pool of blood with its deep burgundy color. She had a lighter hue for the drapes and they had stained the furniture mahogany.

I walked over to the bed and set her down gently, and Jon dimmed the lights.

"You should lie beside her, and I'll take you through a regression while we wait for her to wake." He smiled. "If you need help to relax…" He ran his hand softly in circles on my ass cheek. "I can do a special method for you."

My cock liked that idea.

"Why are you so curious about who I was?"

He nuzzled my neck and ran his forked tongue up to my ear. "I know *who* you *were*. It's time for you to see the truth."

"For the record, I think this is ridiculous." One of his arms reached around me, stroking my ever-growing cock through the jeans. "Mmmm." I relaxed into his embrace.

"Get on the bed." He stepped back, letting me walk around the bed to stretch out.

I kicked my shoes off and sat down on the edge, taking a few deep breaths before lying back and stretching out.

My head bounced on the pillow twice to get it fluffed for my head and I folded my hands on my chest.

"I'm ready."

His rich laughter helped me relax, and then she climbed beside me, stretching out to touch my body with his. He covered my hands with his and I felt his warm breath on the shell of my ear tickling it.

"All I need is for you to relax." His soothing voice murmured in my ear. "Listen to my words, breathe in two, three, four and release that breathe slowly." His thumb stroked the sensitive area on the side of my wrist as he continued.

"You're doing great. Let's do that again. Deep breath in and hold it." I felt his chest move with mine. "And on the exhale, let out the anger, rage and disgust."

I tried to push it all out, and I followed his breathing instructions for three more reps, feeling my body grow heavy like the feeling right before you fall asleep.

"With this next breath, I want you to give in and let the spirits guide you. Follow them as they lead you through the maze of doubt and disbelief."

Right? Someone is going to appear... Wait. Who is that? I felt my eyes squinting at the ethereal woman ahead of me, and the giant hedges that sprouted up before me. She motioned me forward, and I felt my feet moving.

"Wait!" I called out to her and ran to catch up, darting around a corner and falling against the thorny bush. Pain shot through my arm, but I ignored it and tried to catch up.

When I rounded the next corner, the hedges were gone and, in their place, dark brick walls stood. I stopped moving and looked around to see tapestries on the walls and torches to light the corridor. Stepping closer, I reached out and felt the cold brick beneath my fingertips, and the rough material of the hanging.

As I looked left, the long hallway continued, and as I looked to the right, I saw stairs. I spun on my heel and felt something swish around my body. Changing my direction, I walked down the hall and looked inside the first room I came to.

A large candelabra stood near a mirror by the window.

Perfect!

As my image came into view, I patted and fingered the materials as I walked closer to it.

"I'm wearing my grandma's couch!" There was confusion on my face as I inspected the heavy brocade material. Deep red, with gold embroidery and judging by the building, I'm inside a castle.

My jeans were gone and in their place were some puffy shorts, over long stockings. My shoes were leather with small heels.

Where the hell am I?

My t-shirt had been replaced with a white long-sleeved dress shirt and over that a vest that matched my shorts. My cloak had caused the swishing.

The face staring back at me had a long pointy nose, thin lips and a beard, but those were my eyes looking out.

Taking a deep breath, I left the room and walked down the hall to their stairs. My heels making a clickity-clack with each step down. *How annoying.*

At the bottom of the stairs, the servants were running around. None of them made eye contact with me. They bustled around, appearing busy as I entered. An enormous table sat in the middle, two fireplaces flanked it and I took a deep breath, deciding where to go next.

The scent in the room reminded me of last night in the basement, but underneath that, I smelled something wet, moldy and mostly unpleasant.

I decided to just walk and let my feet take me where they wanted. I left the large room and went down a smaller hall which lead to the kitchen.

There stood a fat old lady with her sleeves rolled up, kneading dough. She glanced up and continued her work for a moment before her eyes went wide and she curtsied.

"Sorry, M'Lord. Are you looking for the Lady of the manor?"

I blinked a couple times, realizing I understood her.

"I am." My deep voice resonated in the kitchen.

Her crooked old finger pointed at a door and I dipped my head in thanks before walking through the kitchen to see where the door would take me.

Torches lined the wall on my descent into what I gathered would be a dungeon area and when I hit the bottom of the stairs, *the exact same feeling* washed over me as it did last night when I came upon Anna and the others.

Two of the women bowed to me, and I recognized them as servants. But when the third woman turned, showing me she had a nipple grasped between what looked like pliers, her dark eyes met mine.

A sly smile passed along her face. *"Welcome home, husband. Have you come to play?"*

My dick sprung up tenting my shorts, and I walked over to the small tray of toys, picking up two sewing needles. I wrapped my arms around my wife and felt her plush ass rub against my erection as I slide a needle through the nipple she held out.

The man on the hook screamed into his gag, and my wife shimmied in excitement. *"More."*

I stuck the other needle in creating an x, and looking at one servant, I growled. "Say my name."

"Yes, Count Bathory?"

I sat up straight in the bed, gasping for air. *Now I understood.*

Dominick

"Dom?" Anna scooted over and rubbed my back. "Are you okay?"

I whipped my head her way, looking into the dark pools that bore no fear from my outburst, and slammed my lips against hers.

She's mine. She's always been mine.

Her tongue pushed into my mouth, wrestling with mine, and she maneuvered herself to straddle my lap. She pumped her hips, grinding against my cock, and I slide my hands under her shirt.

My hands cupped her breasts, and I dug my fingers in, eating her moans.

I broke our kiss and panted out. "Naked. On my cock."

"Yesssssssss." She hissed and ripped her shirt up over her head.

My mouth descended on a nipple, sucking and pulling at it until my mouth slipped off and I kissed my way to the other one.

Hands came between us undoing my jeans, and I realized I needed to let her go so we could get naked. With a last nip at her tender peak, I let her go, and she rolled to the side to shed her pants and Jon pushed me back to yank my jeans off my body.

I sat back up and tore my shirt from my body and narrowed my eyes at him. "I want our demon tonight. You can be your sexy man form later."

"My pleasure!" He jumped off the bed and in a shimmering moment, his skin darkened, and his tail grew, whipping around from side to side. "This what you want?" He jumped onto the bed in a catlike pose and crawled up my body. "You like my smooth skin and my tongue."

"Fuck. Yeah." I growled as he pushed me back again and held my legs up and open.

His forked tongue tickled and wiggled around my pelvis, down to my sack and then lower to pierce my asshole. My body tightened and lifted from the bed as he fucked my ass by plunging it in and out. His hand wrapped around my dick and stroked up over my head to collect the pre-cum and back down, rubbing it in.

"You wanted to ride me, Anna. You better get ready. Once I make you come, you're going to be the meat in our sandwich."

"Keep sweet talking me." She panted. "I'm so wet already."

Jon pulled his tongue from my ass and sat back, holding his hands up. Anna wasted no time climbing back onto my lap and sliding down my pole. She cried out and lifted herself up, then undulated her hips, fucking me with shallow strokes.

My hands grabbed her hips, and I bucked my hips up hard, making her scream.

"You..." She wheezed. "Bottomed out."

"Hehe." I winked at her and bounced us on the bed, bumping her cervix each time. "Tonight is my night." She moaned and rode my dick the way I wanted. "That's my good girl."

Jon pushed her forward to lie on me and smiled at me. "Need to get her ready." He held up a plug, and I nodded. "Open up." He purred.

Anna opened her mouth and stuck her tongue out as he placed the metal plug on her tongue and pulled it into her mouth, getting it wet. He pulled it out, and I felt her motions slow as he slid it in place.

My hand slapped her ass. "Ride me."

"Yes, sir." She sat back up and braced her hands on my chest. Her nails bit into my skin and shivered.

"You're mine, Anna." I popped my hips up and smiled. "I want to kill that cocksucker and fuck in celebration."

"We can do that." She slammed her hips back.

"I want to watch Hugh and Ollin fuck you."

She nodded and shivered. "Embracing your darkness, love?"

"Yeah. I'm done fighting it."

She slowed her movements, and I felt her tremble. "Oh no. You're not done."

"So." She gasped. "Close."

"I know." I grabbed her hip and thrust up into her wetness. "You can come, because then the real party begins." Now I slammed into her repeatedly like a machine, making her howl and feeling her cunt soak my cock, balls and drip between my legs.

I chuckled as she sat up straight and shivered from her toes to her head and collapsed over on my chest. Jon moved in, pulled her plug out and I felt him pushing inside her ass. Everything felt stretched tight and our cocks rubbed against each other with a thin wall separating the holes.

"This feels so good." I groaned and tightened a fist in hair, yanking her head back to bite her neck. The bright metallic taste of her blood hit my tongue, and I stroked the spot, enjoying the taste of her.

Jon grabbed her hips and moved her on my cock, keeping his dick tucked deep inside her ass. Moans rumbled in my chest and Anna made small whimpering moans, alternating our names.

"Mm, Dom." She shivered and moved her hips without being directed. "Jon. Oh."

I spread my legs wide so Jon could kneel between them, and I felt something familiar poke against my hole. "Oh, yeah." I groaned and felt his tail push into my ass, connecting us all together.

My mouth pulled from her neck. "Calling a demon of lust to serve was such a wonderful thing, Anna."

"Glad you think so." She leaned forward, laying completely on me, and bit my chest.

"Fuck!" I bucked up on the bed and tightened my ass cheeks around Jon's tail.

"Ungh!" Jon thrust against her ass and I felt Anna's pussy tighten around my dick.

"This feels so good. I don't want it to end." I leaned my head back and moaned as I felt her sucking on my skin.

Jon laughed. "This is only the beginning, my handsome Count."

"I'm calling off tomorrow." The bed helped bounce me deep into her core.

I felt her breathing change, and I knew she wouldn't be able to hold out much longer. Jon nodded, and I felt him offset thrusting making it so between her holes only one would be full at a time.

Anna released her bite and howled. "You beast."

My body felt like an amplifier for Jon's laughter and we both thrusted harder. Her pussy contracted, milking me. I felt her juice dripping, and I didn't want to hold back anymore.

"Oh! Fuck! Anna!" I grunted and slammed her hips down one last time as my cock erupted inside her.

Something buzzed in the room and soon Jon thrust a last time as he exploded deep in her ass and collapsed over onto her back.

"Can we roll?" I wheezed out from the weight.

Anna laughed. "I don't think I have bones left in my body."

"On three." Jon panted. "One, two, three." And together we rolled to the side, with Anna between us.

Her lips brushed against mine, Jon took turns rubbing each of our sides and pressed kisses along her shoulder. The three of us stayed connected, basking in the aftermath of sex. For the first time in my life, I felt like I found where I belonged.

I don't know how much time passed, and none of us cared. Anna enjoyed being snuggled between us and fell asleep.

Not to be a creep, but I studied her face as she slept. Countess Bathory was pretty, but Anna? She's gorgeous.

"Shower?" Jon asked softly.

I nodded, and we carefully untangled limbs and pulled away from Anna. We slipped from the bed and made our way to the bathroom silently.

Jon got the water ready and motioned for me to step inside the large standing shower. The strategically placed water spouts made it so anyone in the shower could get wet. Even if there were up to five or six people.

"This is huge!" I turned in a circle, checking it all out.

The floor felt like it scrubbed your feet and the rocks used for the walls made me feel like I was bathing outside.

"Anna likes to play in the shower." He laughed. "Turn around."

Jon washed my back, ass, down my legs and then had me turn around to wash my front. No playing. No goofing around. All business, but his hands massaged my body as he went, and I felt the stress from the day being washed away.

"Jon? Is Anna immortal?"

He stopped and looked me in the eye. "Yes." He nodded. "Most of Castle Hollow is."

My eyes popped wide open. "No shit?"

"No shit." He smiled. "The ones who are, know who they are and embrace life on their terms. Castle Hollow itself is supernatural."

"So they have to stay here?"

He nodded.

"I want to be immortal with her." I felt my cheeks get hot. "And you."

"Then we will make that happen." He leaned in and kissed my lips softly as the door opened.

"Too late for one more?" Anna yawned as she stepped in and we both reached for her.

"Never too late."

Anna

My shoulders shook as I flipped some bacon over with my titters.

The ghost hunters checked out in the middle of the night. They showed up around three in the morning scared shitless! All I could get from them as they were fleeing was that they saw a bat-like-man.

I shouldn't laugh. It wasn't nice of Jon to spook them, but when you're a demon who's been around since the dawn of time, it's not too far-fetched to develop a hobby of scaring the shit out of people.

The first time he showed me his true form, I felt honored, not scared. Large wings similar to a bat, tail, horns, muscles.

"Hm, we should have him take that form when we pick up Sean."

"Who?" Dom asked, entering the kitchen.

I turned from the stove and looked at him. "Jon."

He padded barefoot to me and wrapped his arms around my middle. "What form?"

Laughter made me shake again. "His full demonic form. He scared the ghost hunters in the woods last night."

"Is that what all the banging was about in the middle of the night?" His lips nibbled my neck.

"Yes." A soft moan slipped out. "Still calling off today?"

"Uh-huh." He pressed his erection into my ass. "I feel like a randy teenager."

I slid the pan off the open burner and shut it off before turning in his arms. "There are worse things to be."

"Indeed." His lips covered mine, and we pecked three times before our mouths opened for our tongues to touch.

Short, quick jabs, teasing each other before I opened more to let him in. Our tongues swirled with each other and he nipped my bottom lip before pulling away.

The chime went off and the front door slammed. The sound of heavy booted feet echoed through the quiet of the inn and soon Hugh, Ollin, and four other men entered the kitchen.

"We need to talk." Hugh took a hard stance, showing off his strong law enforcement side in full uniform, and a gun on his hip.

Ollin and the others had shotguns and stood in an arc around Hugh.

"We do." I smiled. "Gentlemen, please stow the weapons. I made breakfast and added the leaf to the table. There are plans to make."

They all did as asked and set their weapons aside before grabbing a plate and loading up on food.

"Dom, get some food," I pulled from his arms. "I'll go get Jon."

I ran up the stairs and met him in the hall. He lifted me and spun me around, giggling like a little girl.

"What has you so happy?" I giggled with him.

He set me on my feet, cupped my face, and kissed me tenderly. "I have my family back."

"Jon, it's only been forty-eight hours!"

He stopped and looked me in the eye. "Anna, I've known you both since the fifteen hundreds. He knows who he is now, and he's embracing it."

I smiled. "You're right." I took his hand and pulled him down the hall to the stairs. "Let's go. We have plans to make!"

We came down the stairs bouncing and we both loaded up some food on a plate and took a seat at the table.

"Dom? Have you met everyone?" I asked, before taking a bite of bacon.

Hugh cleared his throat. "We all tucked into the food, Anna."

I laughed and went around the table. "You remember Hugh Lincoln, the sheriff? And Ollin Graves, Owner of The Salty Chef."

Dom nodded as he chewed what was in his mouth.

"Beside Ollin is Anton Silva. He's the local mechanic. Next to him is the chief of staff at Eden Memorial Hospital, Doctor Gustavo Frangulin. Sitting beside you is Tristan White, our undertaker, and finally at the other end of the table is Elliot Tucker. He's the mayor."

I watched as he paused with the fork almost to his mouth and narrowed his eyes at Gustavo. "Frangulin?"

"Yes."

"Frankenstein?"

"Not in the lifetime." Gus smiles proudly. "It's Frangulin now."

"Well, I'll be damned."

Jon laughed. "Not yet, you're not!"

Laughter broke out, and everyone finished eating and making small talk. The inn felt alive again. It hasn't felt this way since Gran passed. I didn't want to let her go, but she insisted it was time to go back to the earth and take another spin.

She should come back soon. I missed that old woman!

Ollin wiped his mouth and set his napkin down. "Anna, when should we shoot for? We need to know when before we make our move."

"I would suggest the next full moon." I shrugged and looked at Dom, who tensed in his seat. "Hear me out. The full moon is the best time for blood rituals, and it is the most powerful."

"Damn, she's right." Anton nodded. "That would give us time to dose him."

"Dose him?" Dom looked around at all of us.

Jon smiled at him. "We can get a potion mixed up that can be slipped to him to induce hallucinations, dreams." He shrugged. "Whatever we want."

Hugh pushed his plate forward and leaned on the table. "Which means we'd need you to stay close to him, Dom."

"I'm with you so far." He nodded. "But then what?"

"His meat's too tainted for the diner." Ollin grimaced. "Tristan? You could take care of it?"

"Oh, yeah." Tristan's eyes narrowed. "I might like to use his corpse too before I turn it to ash."

Dom's head slowly turned to me and he mouthed, "necrophilia?"

I lifted my right shoulder in a casual shrug and looked at Anton. "You could handle the car?"

"Awe, yeah." He grinned. "No way anyone will ever find that car."

"And this is how we protect our own." Elliott nodded. "Is this man one of us?" He pointed at Dom.

"I say he is." Jon got up and cleared the dirty dishes from the table. "Last night he remembered who he is."

"Who?" Ollin sat forward. "I wanna know if I'm right."

I laughed. "Gentlemen meet Count Bathory."

Ollin held out his hand to Tristan. "You owe me a c note!"

Tristan leaned to the side and pulled his wallet out while shaking his head. "Dammit."

Dom laughed with everyone and then nodded to Ollin. "I have to know. Who are you?"

"I'm Ollin Graves." He winked. "The earliest I can remember takes me back to the early fifteen hundreds. I believe they called me Ranulf back then. My village burned me at the stake for eating a child." He sighs. "Fools. The village was starving."

Dom looked at his lap and then lifted his head and took a deep breath. "I'm a serial killer. The first kill was completely an accident. The next four weren't."

Everyone sat back and waited. The floor was his, and we wanted the story.

He laughed. "Sex is fun, but I love when it's rough. Dirty. Hard. Painful. And sometimes I get carried away." Dom shrugged. "My brother owns a pig farm and has helped me out."

Around the table, coffee cups lifted and Ollin gave the toast. "One of us!"

Dom lifted his cup as well and we all clinked, yelling out, "ONE OF US!"

"So we have a plan. Anna, can you mix up a potion?" Ollin asked.

"You bet your wrinkled ass I can."

"Last I remember, you ate my wrinkled ass out, so stuff it." He laughed. "Anton will handle the car. Tristan can have the tainted meat." Ollin looked at Gustavo. "Do you need a cadaver for anything?"

"You know, I have some young female trainees coming in. He'll be perfect for them to cut apart before Tristan discards him."

Dom laughed. "If I didn't know better, I'd think you have done this before."

I looked at him and nodded. "We take care of our own."

"Can you handle being close to him for the next month?" Hugh pinned Dom with a stare.

"Oh yeah. I gave a young girl my word he wouldn't hurt anyone else."

"Thank you for the reminder!" I laughed. "I'll make sure that not only does he have hallucinations, but he won't be able to get it up at all."

Tristan thumbed to Dom. "Does he know how full moon rituals end?"

"How?" Dom looked around nervously.

Hugh and Ollin barked out laughter together before Hugh answered. "With sex, of course!"

A devious smile crept across Dom's face. "Perfect."

Dominick

After everyone left, Anna took me into her private pantry and showed me how she mixed potions and hex bags. Then showed me her special book she made from a peasant when we were the Count and Countess.

I read through some spells and sat there dumbfounded. With this book, it hit me she could be unstoppable.

"What stops you from doing whatever you want?" I flipped another page.

"Dominick." She turned to face me and cocked her hip to the side with her hand on it. "I have *some* morals. The girls I sacrifice, no one misses."

"Anna, I came here asking about them. Someone was missing them?"

"Who?"

"What do you mean, who?" I shook my head.

"Who filed the missing person report?" She smiled.

I thought back to the files and realized none of them were done by family members and the common link was the ages. They all were between nineteen and twenty-one. I felt my jaw slacken, and I shook my head.

"No." I blew out a breath. "Are you telling me they're all connected?"

She nodded and opened a jar on the table, taking a pinch of the dry ingredient and sprinkling it over the others in the bowl she had in front of her. "Do the math, Dom."

I closed the book and set it on the table. "You done?"

Her head fell back in laughter. "No, but you could do something to hurry this along."

"Name it."

"Get on your knees and crawl to me." Her dark eyes shimmered.

I felt my eyebrow raise.

"On." The smile left her face. "Your." She turned her body to me. "Knees." Her manicured nail pointed to the floor. "Dominick."

I slid from the stool I'd been sitting on and dropped to the floor. "Are you using magic?"

"Does it feel like I am?" She tilted her head and anger flashed across her face.

I crawled to her. "No."

"Take my pants off."

I kissed my way up to her waist. "Yes, mistress."

Her fingers brushed through my hair, and she grabbed a handful and yanked my head back. "You look handsome on your knees before me."

My fingers hooked into the waistband of her leggings, and I pulled them down slowly and waited for her next command.

"Such a good boy." She purred and stepped out of them, shoving my head lightly. "Now. I'm going to finish this potion, and you?" Anna turned back to her table. "You eat my pussy. And don't be shy about. I want to feel your tongue fucking me."

My cock pressed uncomfortably against the confines of my jeans. "Can I jack off?"

"No." She spread her legs to allow me access. "You have one job. Now get to it."

I moved between her legs and brought my mouth up to warm, wet lips. My nose nuzzled her soft hair before my tongue pushed between them, tasting her honey.

My hands reached up to hold her hips, and she swayed.

"No hands. Only your mouth."

I chuckled and put my hands down, nipping at her wet lips before spearing my tongue inside. My nose rubbed against her clit and I shook my head, treating it like a dog with a chew toy, smearing her juice all over my face.

"Mm, Dominick. That's good." She widened her legs and humped my face.

I hadn't shaved in three days and I knew my stubble added to the effect, scratching and prickling her sensitive skin.

"Such a good boy." She purred. "That feels so good."

Her soft moans and words spurred me on, as I flattened my tongue and lapped from inside her core to her bundle of nerves where my lips locked around it, sucking it further out from its hood. My teeth bit down gently between each pull of my suction, making her legs tremble.

She slipped down, spreading her legs more, her hands slapping down on the table.

I rolled my head as my tongue wriggled all over and in her, and got my shoulders behind her legs, leaning my head as far back as I could.

Her moans and words sounded muffled now that her thighs blocked my ears. "Ikuor, cilipasub yckuanu phuq pkulo aiueau!"

I doubled my effort, using my entire face and mouth to eat her sweet pussy. Anna moaned louder and rode my face harder.

"Dom!" she panted. "Fuck! So good."

I felt like a machine as I repeated my lapping and rubbing. Her hips shimmied down and her hand pounded the table.

"Mm. Mmm. Mmmm." She went up on her tiptoes and her legs shook as she cried out. "AhhhHHHhh! Ahhhhhh!"

Her body tightened, and I reached up to hold her hips as her orgasm rolled through her. I swore there was a dam inside her and it busted wide open as I lapped up as much as I could and let the rest coat my face and drip down my chin.

Her thighs closed around my head, holding it between the pillowy softness of her skin. Once she could breathe again, she released my head and laughed.

"So sorry." She shivered with an aftershock. "Didn't mean to try to kill you."

I laughed with her. "What a way to go!"

Anna stepped back so I could stand up and looked around the table while stretching my neck muscles. "Is it ready?"

"Yep." She sighed and leaned against me. "All you need to do is dose him once a day when you see him."

"Do you need to do anything more here?" I wrapped my arm around her. She shook her head, and I smiled. "Good." I scooped her up and took her upstairs to our room.

Making love all day was the best way I can think of spending a day. My body wasn't in agreement. I felt like an old man. My body ached from my toes to my hair, but I had no plans to give up sex, so my muscles better take notice and get with the program.

I ran through the drive thru at the local fast-food joint and grabbed 2 coffees. When I got to the station, I added the potion Anna made and swirled the cup the mix it in. Then I took both and went inside.

It always jarred my senses to go from the peacefulness outside to the noisy hustle and bustle of the station. I'd been a cop since I turned twenty and went into the police academy. Maybe after this it was time to change professions?

They clustered together desks around the room and I wound my way through them to the back, where Sean and I shared that office.

I set his coffee on his desk and went around to my desk, pulling out my new chair and sitting down. It still felt weird that a seat would mold to ass, but I couldn't deny the comfort.

Flipping on my computer, I waited for it to wake up and go through all the processes while I read over the small stack of pink message papers on my desk. As I checked the dates and times, it occurred to me that Sean should've been here to respond to some of them.

So why wasn't he here during that time? He told me he was coming back to the station.

I heard his off-key whistling and took a deep breath, knowing I had a part to play.

"Howdy, partner!" He came in and pull out his chair, flopping into it. "Coffee? Is it my birthday?"

"Shut up." I joked. "I buy you coffee."

"I know." He smiled. "So, did you get her out of your system?"

"Get who out of my system?" I asked, drinking my coffee.

"The Bishop chick. She was snooty." He sat forward and picked up the coffee. "But she was eyein' you, man. I was hoping maybe you hit it to forget it."

Sitting back in my chair, I tilted my head. "You feeling okay?"

"Better than I have in weeks." He shrugged.

"The wife give you some?" I teased.

Sean winked at me, took a drink of the coffee and smiled. "Sure. We'll go with that."

Keep it together, Dominick. You have twenty-eight more days to go. And you can't shoot him inside the station.

"How'd you like that diner yesterday?" *If I couldn't hurt him yet, I could at least enjoy the fact that he ate long pig and loved it.*

"Damn. That was some gooooooood barbeque. We should go there again."

"Yeah." I nodded. "We could do that." I split up the messages and tossed half onto his desk. "Divide and conquer time."

"Let's do it." He laughed and tilted his head back, draining his coffee.

1 week later

I spent the weekend with Anna and Jon in bed and this time I felt like a god. No muscle aches, no lack of sleep. Just good old-fashioned fucking and eating.

Parking my car, I doctored his coffee and took both cups in. I steeled myself for the switch from peace to noise and ended up pleasantly surprised when the bull was much tamer than it had been in previous weeks.

The captain gave me a nod as I walked by his office, making my way to the back, where Sean had his head on the desk.

"You look rough, man." I set his coffee down. "Long weekend?"

"Weird week." He groaned and sat up. "Thanks for the coffee." He lifted it to hip lips. "Where do you get it from? I really like the taste."

"The fast-food place between here and Castle Hollow." I took a drink from mine. "I agree. They made decent coffee."

"Moody." He leaned forward. "Are you *still* hittin' that?"

I can't wait to pull your fingernails off one at a time.

"Yeah. Bed's comfy, food's good, and the pussy can keep up." I deadpanned.

"Just don't go movin' in." He laughed and looked at his wristwatch. "Hey, we're due up to the elementary in an hour to talk to the little ones."

Fuck! I forgot about this meeting.

"You can stay here since you're whipped." My shoulders lifted in a shrug. "I can handle a few classes of crotch goblins."

He sat back, taking another drink of his coffee. "Yeah, I could do. I'm better with teens than little ones with their sticky hands and boogers."

You son of a bitch, you probably justify it by saying if she's old enough to bleed, she's old enough to breed.

"Sounds like a good plan." I nodded. "You can finish typing up some reports. I did my share."

"Man, I am exhausted." He yawned.

Picking up my desk phone, I dialed his house.

"Sean?" His wife answered.

"Hey there, Kenzie, it's Dom."

"Oh, hello!" She giggled into my ear. "What? What can I do for you?" She dropped her voice to a lower pitch, and I narrowed my eyes.

What the fuck is going on?

"Sean's barely awake at his desk. I'm going to drop him off at home on my way to a presentation and I'll even pick him up in the morning."

"That's sweet."

"You just make sure he gets some sleep, okay?" I tapped on my desk.

"Sure." Her voice went flat. "I'll do that."

I hung up the receiver and looked at my partner with a smile. "C'mon sleeping beauty, time to go home and catch up on sleep."

"I'm older than you." He reminded me.

"And?" I gave him a friendly bump in his arm. "You can't work or drive like that."

"Fine." Sean grumbled and drained his coffee. "Let's go."

We slipped out the backdoor and I felt victorious inside. *I'm keeping him away from kids and he has no way to go anywhere. Whatever Anna put in the potion is working.*

Once we got to my sedan, I jokingly opened the door for him and he scowled, but got in. I did a small fist pump and walked around to get in on my side.

I waited until we were a way from the station before I tried talking to him. "Is everything okay at home?"

He yawned again. "What? Oh, yeah." Sean half shrugged. "I just... haven't been sleeping well. You ever go through times like that?"

"Yeah." I nodded. "Happens to all of us at sometime."

"I guess." He yawned again and his head fell back against the seat rest.

This might work and we'll make it the full four weeks. I glanced over at Sean and in place of the bile that had been rising, I felt anger and excitement.

I can't wait to see you on the hook begging you miserable cock.

Dominick

I pulled up to Sean's house and honked my horn to signal my arrival. He stumbled out of the front door, looking more disheveled than he had the previous day.

When he opened the door and climbed inside, I shook my head. "What happened? You were supposed to rest."

"Man." He sighed and threw his head back against the headrest. "Every time I fell asleep, all I saw were demons and hell and weird shit."

"Maybe you need to go to confession?" I pulled away from the curb and drove down the street.

He chuckled. "Maybe. Ain't got nothing to confess, though."

I can't wait to cut out your lying tongue.

Sean reclined the seat. "Hey man, don't forget to get coffee."

"Don't worry, Sean, I won't, I can tell you really need it." I turned at the end of the road and drove towards the place I'd been stopping.

He had his phone out and hid the screen from my peripheral, which added fuel to the fire already burning in my mind.

How long has he been preying on young girls? How has he not been caught?

His phone pinged with a new message, and I couldn't resist asking. "Who ya talking to?"

"What? Are you my wife now?" He laughed. "Look, we've been partners for five years, but we've never really pried into each other's personal life."

My thumbs tapped on the steering wheel.

He's right, we never have. It's been all petty details and talk. He'd always been closed off, and I never pressed the issue. I figured that's why we made an excellent team. No personal feelings to contend with.

I nodded my head towards the restaurant. "That's where I've been going."

"I always forget that place is there. It's just such a rinky dink place." He nodded and set his phone face down on his leg and closed his eyes.

How could I get the potion into his coffee today?

Lost in my own thoughts, I drove around the building and ordered two coffees. One with cream and sugar and the other black. The woman had me pull around and gave me the coffees, wishing me a good day.

"Wait." Sean squinted at me. "She didn't charge you."

"She said she give the police a freebie on coffee." I took a sip of the bitter brew and then put it in my drink holder to continue to the station.

Sean sipped his and played on his phone until I parked. I appreciated the quiet, but I hated thinking he was up to no good on his phone.

We exited the car and walked side by side into the station, and my skin crawled the entire way. Waiting twenty-seven more days felt unbearable.

The bullpen seemed back to normal today, loud shouts, drawers slamming and some vagrant informing the one female officer we had that he needed to piss assaulted my ears and I decided that after we took care of dumb nuts, I would find a different place to work.

Once we got to our office, he put his coffee down and excused himself, which gave me the ideal opportunity to dose his coffee. I peered out the window to make sure he wasn't in sight and that nobody else was coming, then I poured it in and swished it around.

On my desk sat a pink note.

To: Detective Moody

From: Liz Callahan

I'd like to talk to you about my daughter.

"What's that?" Sean asked, walking back into the office and sitting at his desk.

"It's from the Callahan woman. She wants to talk to me about her daughter."

Sean's head snapped up. "What?"

I shrugged. "I'll call her and stop by on my way home."

"Kilton is out of the way. We should go this afternoon."

My head tilted, and I lifted my eyes to peer at him over the note. "It's not that far from Castle Hollow and if something happened with her daughter, I don't mind going to talk to them."

His face paled, and he shook his head. "Nah, let's go after lunch. We can grab a bite at that place near the inn."

"The Salty Chef?" I scrunched up my face. "I don't feel like meat today."

"So get a salad." He reached for his coffee. "Then we'll go talk to her about her dead daughter."

He's keeping track of the girls. Play it cool, Moody.

"The daughter is dead?" I took a seat and folded my hands on my desk.

His eyes widened and went back to normal as he nodded and swallowed hard. "Yeah. It was in the papers."

"Damn. I should've noticed that." I sat back and sighed. "What happened? Was it an accident?"

"The obit never said." He shrugged.

Uh-huh. I nodded. "Well, I guess we'll do it your way."

"I do have more experience." He grinned.

I'll bet you do. Fucker.

After that comment, I needed to ignore him and focus on anything but torturing his body into a lifeless corpse. "Hey give me one of those reports you need done."

"Gladly." He tossed one over to me and I tucked into my work for the next four hours.

Sometime later, the captain knocked on our door. "Hey guys. What have you learned about the Bishop case?"

Sean leaned back and tapped his pen against his lips. "Nothing."

"Nothing?" He raised an eyebrow.

I shook my head. "Miss Bishop told me what she remembered, and it matched the reports done."

"Keep looking." He shook his head, muttering under his breath as he walked away.

"You ready for lunch?" Sean smiled and seemed more awake.

I glanced at the clock and nodded. "Sure."

"Let's drive separate." He stretched and stood up. "That way, if we're with the Callahan's for a while, we can just go home."

"Sure." I stood up. "Let's go."

Liz Callahan called and left *me* a message. Since he left in his car, I pulled the note from my pocket and called her from my car as I pulled out of the parking lot.

The phone rang three times before she answered and her voice sounded shaky. "Missus Callahan? This is detective Moody."

"You got my message?" She sniffled.

"I did." I turned onto the road and headed towards Ollin's diner.

"Does your partner know I called?" She whispered.

"Yes, but he's not with me at the moment."

A sob filled my ear. "I can't see him."

"What happened?"

"I found my daughter's dairy." She partially growled. "And I know why she committed suicide."

Shit. Shit. Shit.

"I'll come alone." I assured her.

She sniffled more. "Good. I'll turn it over to you." She blew her nose in my ear and I pulled over to the side of the road. "I can't tell my husband. He'll kill him and I can't lose them both."

"I promise you. I understand."

"Thank you."

There was a soft click in my ear, and I knew the call had been disconnected. *You gotta love old phones.* I looked down at my phone and dialed the sheriff.

"Lincoln." His gruff voice filled my ear.

"The girl who took her life? Her mom found her diary." I pinched the bridge of my nose. "We're doing lunch at Ollin's."

He chuckled. "I'll assemble the troops."

I ended the call and finished driving to The Salty Chef.

Sean Riley

I couldn't wait to get to that damn diner. All I could think about on my drive was the beautiful waitress from last time.

Her soft blond hair, tender skin and her mouth. Her mouth did things to me that curled my toes. She was a little older than I liked, but oh so innocent.

I loved being the older man who taught the girls how men like things. The right words, a few hugs, being attentive to their words and then they're moldable putty in my hands.

"Mm." I moaned and stroked the limp dick in my pants. "Hollie was one of the sweetest." I remembered her crying on my shoulder after the break in. Her face buried against my neck. Her soft perfume.

Maybe I can get the mom to let me see her room so I can snag something to remember her by other than my memories?

"Damn!" I slammed my hands on the steering wheel. "Why can't I get it up?!" Growling in anger, I turned off the road and pulled into the parking lot for the diner. "No matter. I can get some good food and have something pretty to look at."

Getting out of my car, I looked around to see if Moody had arrived yet, but his car wasn't in the lot and I didn't see any cars coming up the road. *Ah, well, I'm going in.*

I walked up the small sidewalk up to the glass doors and entered, smiling when I saw a blond. The moment she turned and saw me, she dropped the plate in her hands, gasping.

She seemed familiar. Then it hit me. *Miss Pumpkin, who went to the movies alone.*

The old man came from the back and walked over to her. "Take a break, dear. I got this."

"Yes, sir." Her sweet voice made me smile, and I sauntered to the back table we sat at last time.

I watched as she walked around the wall and down the hall and instead of sitting down; I followed her down the hall. When I got to the doors for the bathrooms, she wasn't there.

Looking over my shoulder to make sure no one else came this way, I gave the women's bathroom doorknob a twist, smiling when it wasn't locked. I slipped inside and my smile disappeared, seeing an immense man standing there.

"You, Riley?" His gruff voice reverberated off the walls.

I moved my jacket, showing off my shoulder holster. "Who the fuck wants to know?"

"Good enough for me." His fist connected with my face and everything went black.

"Come on." *Tap. Tap. Tap.* "Time to wakey-wakey." A woman's voice filtered into my ear.

My arms felt like they were being pulled up off my body and my feet? I moved them around and could only stand on the balls of my feet.

Why am I cold?

I blinked my eyes a few times and slowly things came into focus. The Bishop woman stood before me with a smile on her face.

"There he is!"

I looked down and saw why I felt cold, and she laughed.

"About now is when you should realize you're at a distinct disadvantage."

I gave my arms a jerk, which sent my body into a swaying motion, moving my feet from the floor and pulling harder on my shoulders.

"Tsk-tsk." She shook her head. "It's the first thing everyone tries and since I know what a bastard you are, I'll let you in on a little secret." She giggled and stepped closer. "It makes me laugh *every. Single. Time.*"

I snarled at her and tried to lunge, which humored her further. "Bitch!"

"Now, Sean, who do you think will make sure you eat every day?" She gave me a wink. "I can feed you good things or I can feed you shit."

"Anna?" Dom's voice came down the stairs, and I smiled at her as I heard someone coming down the stairs.

"He'll let me go, you crazy bitch."

She turned and ran into his arms once he took a step into the room and he embraced her. "I see he's awake."

"I tired of waiting and gave him some love taps."

He lifted her chin up and kissed her. Their mouths were open, showing me how their wet tongues played together.

"Hey! Dom!" I growled.

With his tongue still twirling with hers, he glanced at me. "Wha?"

"She's got me locked up! Let me go!" I pulled at the chain again and swayed more.

Dom's laughter filled the room, and he stepped away from his whore to come to me. "Oh, Anna, you were right!"

"I'm telling you, it's as if they lose their minds."

I heard footfalls on the steps and I cried out. "Help! Help me!" The weird guy that worked here at the inn came down the stairs with a metal bucket in his hand and the old man from the diner on his heels. "Help!"

The old man looked over, and an evil smile spread across his face. "I brought something special for you."

Dom turned away from me, linked his hand with that bitch's and they left the room. The creepy guy stood behind me and held me in place while the old man went to the bucket and moved something in it before pulling it out.

"Got him?"

"Yes, sir." The man behind me wrapped his arms around mine and held my head still. "He's ready."

"This is for every sweet girl you hurt."

"Wha? What are you?" I saw the red metal of the branding iron as it passed my eyes and lined up with my forehead. "No!" I could feel the heat coming off of it in waves and I tried to move, but the weirdo had some unnatural strength to him.

I felt tears falling down my cheeks. "Stop! I'll be good. I'll…." The searing iron came closer until it connected to my forehead. I heard the sizzle of my flesh before I felt the intense pain which made me scream until my voice faded away and everything went black.

Sean

I felt my piss dribble out and splash on the floor, coating my toes. All the days run into each other and I couldn't tell you how long I've been held captive here. My head limply turns to see my small cage they stick in me to give my arms a break. I've come to crave the cold floor and reprieve.

Does my wife miss me? Is anyone looking for me?

Right now my ass is being stretched for god knows what and I'm missing a nipple. Most of my nails are gone, and they broke all my fingers.

The first day they put me in the cage, a mirror lined the floor and after the door closed, mirrors made up the walls and top. There wasn't anywhere to hide and every time I looked into the mirrors, I could read the word pedophile on my head.

They carved the names of the girls they found out about into my flesh and they made me tell them the names of others to join in the graffiti.

My jaw ached from the gag in my mouth, and my mouth felt dry. I heard footsteps coming down the stairs, and I glanced up to see who my tormentor would be.

Jon looked over at me and smiled. "You poor thing, you must feel so miserable."

I looked up at him, hoping for sincerity.

He walked closer and cupped my face. "Would you feel better if you knew your punishment was almost over?"

My body felt lighter, and I nodded.

"Good." He winked and went around behind me.

I couldn't see what he was doing, but I could hear things moving. He walked around carrying large chaise loungers and removed the dark material from the walls, exposing mirrors all around with one broken.

I heard him drag something on the ground and felt the first blast of cold water hit my body, jarring me.

"You stink!" He yelled over the sound of the water. "Can't have a proper ritual with a stinky pig now, can we?"

The water coated my body, and then a hard scrub brush followed. I don't know if I was so sensitive that it hurt or if he made it purposely hurt. I would bet on the latter. He scrubbed my feet, legs, and ass. Then he loaded the brush up and did my penis and torso. Every cut felt torn open as the soap filled in, making them burn.

And if I thought him to be kind, he proved me wrong when he scrubbed my head and face the same way.

The gag muffled my screams, and then soap made its way into my mouth.

Soon the cold water hit my body again, rinsing the blood and soap away. Then he cleaned the floor and rinsed it clean before he took his leave.

Dominick

The full moon illuminated the sky brilliantly, and tonight was a special night for all of us.

I stepped from the shower and wrapped a towel around my waist after drying off, and went to our room to get dressed.

Anna stood before the mirror in a sheer gown and smiled at my reflection. "Are you sure this is what you want?"

"To be immortal and live with you and Jon and our friends?" I strolled over to her. "Absolutely."

She tilted her head, giving me access to her neck, and I leaned in, biting hard.

"Dom!"

I let go of my bite and licked the wound. "I know you're wet."

"And?" She laughed and slipped from me. "Come downstairs when you're ready."

I would never tire of watching her walk away from me. And tonight I took my place in Castle Hollow.

We didn't have any clients staying at the inn, so I opted to cut out the middleman. Why put on clothes if you're only going to take them off? I pulled my towel from my waist and tossed it into the bathroom, then left our room.

If someone would've told me that one day I would live with a powerful immortal witch and demon in a supernatural city, I'd've laughed and had them committed. Or at least sent someone out to do a welfare check.

Over the last month, I've learned how real the supernatural can be. I've seen magic work. And I've learned to accept people for who they are.

My half-hard cock bounced as I walked down the hall to the stairs that would lead me to the kitchen. We're lucky that table can't talk.

I made a stop at the fridge to grab something to drink, then went to the wall with our secret door. My hand knew where to press, and the wall granted me access. The door closed behind me and I jogged down the stairs, excited to get our night started.

Ollin sat on the same lounger I first saw him on. Hugh had his and Anton sat beside him. Tristan sat across the room with Jon and Anna. And in the center hung Sean.

"You ready to kick things off?" Jon smiled at me.

"I am." I looked back at Sean and walked over to the small table of tools. "You know why this is being done to you, yes?"

He shook his head, and I reached behind his head and unbuckled the gag, removing it.

"You still don't get it, do you?"

His hoarse voice croaked out a reply. "I can change."

"No. You can't." I reached for a small collar. "You knew touching someone young was wrong. Yet you continued." I crouched and secured the spiked collar around his ball sack, letting three thin chains dangle down.

"I could go to therapy!"

"Hm, I think we're a bit past that. Don't you?" I stood up and walked behind him. I picked up some small weighs from the table. We equipped them with hooks to hang on the end of the chains. Crouching down again, I attached them one by one, giving him time to whine and cry between each addition.

As I stood up, I kept my naked form hidden and nodded to Anna.

My woman stood up and walked over in front of him. She lifted her arms up and her voice filled the room. "Gurongiene thoa jiscrai je traich aifpra!"

Hollie Callahan appeared in front of her. "Darling, I called you here to face your tormentor."

The young girl turned, and her eyes moved from his head to his feet. When her eyes came back up, they met mine.

"Did you do this for me?"

"For you and all the other girls." I ripped the asshole stretcher from his ass, causing him to cry out in pain.

"I'm sorry!" He sobbed. "I'm so sorry!"

"You're only sorry you got caught." She shook her head. "Can you send him to hell?"

I smiled at the young girl. "With pleasure."

Anna leaned over to speak into Hollie's ear. "May your spirit be at rest now."

She poofed into the air and Anna stepped closer to Sean. "Would you like to know what happened to my parents, Detective Riley?" He sobbed and shook his head, making Anna laugh. "They decided to keep me from my gran. And then I watched my father hit my mother."

Her hand reached out to the tray and lifted a beautiful dagger. "I came home to punish them for their decision and found them fucking in bed." Her voice turned to ice. "I gave them a chance to speak, but all I heard was bullshit."

After shifting the knife to her right hand, she picked up a tool that was used to hold tongues. She lifted her foot and grabbed a chain between her toes. When Sean howled, she plunged the tongs into his mouth and pulled his tongue out.

"So I cut their lying tongues out." The blade sliced through his tongue, making him choke on his next howl.

"My brave woman." I blew her a kiss and walked around in front of Sean, accepting the dagger from her.

I took a deep breath and placed the blade against his neck. The others stood and formed a circle around us. I lifted my head and said the chant Anna taught me.

"At daluku nue, usthai enca ciili hisii!" Then I pulled the blade across his neck, dropped to my knees, and let his blood cover me.

When the blood flow slowed to a stop, Anton and Hugh took him down and Jon cleared the tray.

Ollin walked over and kissed my cheeks. "Beautiful job, son."

Another set of lips pressed against my neck. "Congratulations." Tristan's soft voice spoke into my ear.

I stood up and my cock bobbed crudely in front of me. Anna wrapped her hand around it and stroked it as she covered my mouth in a kiss. "That was sexy."

I felt Jon at my back. His forked tongue tickled my neck. "So sexy."

Hugh held his hand out and I accepted it, pulling him in for a hug with Anna between us. "What can we do for you?" A sly smile crept along his face.

I slipped out from between Jon and Anna. "On your knees."

Anna slid down to her knees and looked at me for her next command.

"Like a dog in heat." My voice deepened.

She licked her lips and fell forward, catching herself with her hands.

"Good girl, now open your mouth and suck the first cock that goes in."

She tilted her head up and opened her mouth. Jon stepped back and let Tristan go first. He placed it on her tongue and hissed when her mouth closed around him.

"You know what?" I wrapped my hand around my cock and stroked it. "Keep her busy. Hands, mouth, pussy and ass. She's not done until she can't walk."

Anton slid between her legs and moved up so she could push back on him, and Hugh got to his knees behind her. He pulled her cheeks apart and pushed against her tight hole. While those two got their cocks wet, Jon and Ollin each took a side and waited for her to sit up and grab onto their erections.

Seeing my woman used so thoroughly made my cock harder, and I sat back on a lounger. The mirrors let me see everything happening, every thrust. And the sounds in the room were what I pictured heaven would be like.

Most men might be jealous seeing someone else fuck their woman, but for me? Knowing she would do anything for me made me feel like a god.

"Pinch her nipples, Anton. And Hugh? Slap that ass."

Her muffled moans kept a smile on my face, and Tristan had his fist in her hair. His hips bucked wildly as he face-fucked her.

"Where do you want my load? Down her throat?" He groaned. "Or all over her face?"

"Nut on her face. She likes that." I moaned and sank down on the lounger.

Jon looked over his shoulder. "If you come closer, my tail can help you."

"Fuck." A groan rumbled in my chest. "I'm torn between watching and being fucked."

"Anton, I want a crack at that pussy." Ollin panted.

Tristan pulled his cock from her mouth and moaned as he stroked to a finish on her face. Anna moaned, and I walked over and tapped her lips with my dick.

"Keep sucking."

She lapped at my blood covered skin and took me down her throat, holding me there and then pulling off.

"Don't slow down jacking those cocks."

She made a sound around my cock and Anton's toes curled. His moans grew louder and his hips thrust up as his body shook.

"Yeah! Fill her up!" I held her head with both hands. "Isn't this what Jon wanted? To see me hold your head and face-fuck you until you swallow every last drop?"

Jon shivered and winked at me. "Yes." He hissed. "Fuck her pretty face!"

I watched the mirrors and saw Anton slide out, with some finagling, and then Ollin slid beneath her. Hugh lifted her leg to make it easier and when he slid his cock in, he moaned loud.

"Damn, I love a good wet pussy!" His hands reach up and pulled at her nipples.

Her moans vibrated around my cock and I pumped my hips faster. I loved the feel of her mouth sucking me off, and the eager way she swallowed.

"Use your teeth, just a little." I panted and moaned when I felt her teeth tease the top and bottom of my cock. "That's my girl."

Hugh looked over at me and smiled. "I'm blessin' her back!" He pulled from her ass and stroked to his finish shooting not only her back, but me as well. "Sorry, 'bout that."

"We're good." I moaned and thrust in until her nose pressed against the nest of hair at the base of my cock. "Damn, woman, you suck so good." I pulled out and did it repeatedly, each time holding her in place longer.

"Every time you do that, she gushes." Ollin smiled up at me. "Keep it up."

Jon covered her hand with his and took over, jacking himself off. His head fell back and he let the lust wash over him. Over the last month, he taught me how pure lust can be and how dirty sex can get.

"Coat them tits." I encouraged him.

"Oh, I plan to." He grunted, and I watched as his cum exploded in bursts all over her breasts. He stumbled back a few steps and chuckled. "Damn. I love ritual nights." He ambled over to a chaise and flopped down.

Ollin groaned and bucked his hips up. His fingers gripped her slippery nipples, and he twisted them, making her open her throat when she moaned.

"Fuck." He panted. "I just painted her insides." His arms fell away to the sides, and that left me humping her face.

I held my hips still and moved her head. Her tongue worked the underside of my cock and I loved feeling my balls swing to hit her chin.

"I'm so close, baby. You ready?"

I thrust down her throat one last time as she moaned. She swallowed, and I pulled out enough to watch her cheeks puff out with my cum, feeling her lips tighten around me, not letting any escape.

"That's my girl, such a good girl." My toes curled under and my muscles tightened, feeling the orgasm rush through my body.

When my cock stopped throbbing, I pulled from her mouth and let go of her hair, smiling as she collapsed to the floor.

Epilogue

Anna

It's been six months since Detective Sean Riley went missing and not even his wife misses him. She moved on after a month.

We checked in a new group of ghost hunters. Jon's planning to go all wolfman on them tomorrow night. Gotta keep the outsiders on their toes.

And since here in Castle Hollow we take care of our own, today we're celebrating the swearing in of the new undersheriff. Hugh and Dom worked a case together and found they make a hell of a team.

Dom is looking forward to being in town and working with the people here.

Me?

I'm looking forward to our own celebration later.

Ivy Penn is a dark romance author who has a macabre sense of humor and loves horror movies. Growing up as a single child, she was often lonely and began creating characters to entertain herself. She lives in the Midwestern United States with her husband, child, and a dog she affectionately calls her office manager. Her hobbies include drinking coffee, reading, and cooking.

Stories that Bloom

Stalk me!

Indecent Intent

Twisted Truths

Shattered Dreams

Petty Deadly Gorgeous

Dark - Gritty - Omegaverse

Marked by the Alpha

Made in the USA
Columbia, SC
27 February 2025